MW01700443

TROUBLED ISLAND

W.M. PATTERSON

PARDUS
MEDIA

To the people of the islands who unknowingly inspired this story

PROLOGUE

I come from a small island called Inishard which lies ten miles off the north-west coast of the county of Donegal - the most northerly county in Ireland. In the English language 'Inishard' translates as 'High Island'. It was my home for nearly eighty years, and although I don't live there any more, I'm well qualified to tell you a bit about it and the people who choose to live there, despite the hardships that are common to every island community.

Inishard is about three miles long and a mile wide with high cliffs up on the north side and the land slopes down to the sea on the south side. There are just over two hundred Islanders, and most families depend on fishing for a living. Nearly all of us live in what could be called a village on the west side but there are a good number of houses scattered the length of the island.

On stormy days the boats can't leave the island, and in fact we could be cut off for a few days, or even a week or more. People don't like being cooped up anywhere, but especially on a small island, and so the sea has a great bearing on our lives. When it's calm and full of sunshine, that's usually the way we are too, as we head for the mainland for supplies or out to fish for herring or mackerel on the deep dark-blue swelling waters which surround us. Our fishing boats are 30 to 40 feet long with Lister diesel engines.

The 'Mail-boat' is the biggest boat we have, and was built by the Dixon brothers from Tory Island. It's about 42 feet long, and is used exclusively for transporting goods and people to and from island. The cargo often includes livestock, building materials, crates of Guinness and beer, fresh and canned food, ropes, canvas, barrels of oil, in fact anything and everything that is needed to sustain life in a remote community. On calm days we go out in 12-foot boats called curraghs, catching crabs and lobsters closer to the shore. These curraghs are very light and rest on top of the sea like corks, and are easily carried and rowed by two men using long narrow oars. They are made on the island from thin laths or canes reinforcing a strong frame, and covered in canvas which is then tarred on the outside to make them waterproof.

When the weather is dark and stormy for too long, small disputes can become big disputes if there is no outlet for impatience, worry or aggression. To deal with that we have card nights, dances in the pub lounge, nights of story-telling in someone's house or other such diversion while we wait on the weather to return to normal. We're not entirely dependent on fishing as the government helps out by giving each family a few pounds to make sure we won't go hungry when bad weather keeps us ashore. We collect the money, we call it the 'dole', from our own postmaster or postmistress who is also the shopkeeper on the island.

Apart from fishing, there is some common land where we graze a few goats, some sheep and a half dozen cows. We have donkeys and carts for transport. There are no trees on the island, they're long gone, used for fuel and building, way way back in time. When the trees were all cut down our ancestors dug turf from the peat bogs and when that was used up, they gathered sods from between the rocks and dried them for the fire, but that fuel wasn't much good and barely kept the fire alive never mind giving out much heat, but better than nothing. If you come here, you can see where the rocks are all exposed from taking the sods away. Nowadays we bring fuel over from the mainland, bags of coal, turf and logs.

Every year we plant spuds and corn and mix our thin soil with rotting seaweed as fertilizer, and sometimes with some modern factory-made fertilizer. The priest comes to bless the planting and to pray for a good crop, the same as he blesses the boats before they venture out on the dangerous deep. Every island community knows its share of tragedy given the capricious nature of the weather and horizons are scanned by experienced eyes before the decision to go or not is made. Even then, weather can change and our boats can be caught out when far from shore. You can imagine the fear in the hearts of the people, not only in the families of the crews when this happens.

The religion here is Roman Catholic but our Pagan past still resonates despite the passage of over a thousand years, so that while prayers are directed to Christ, the old King-God Balor is often lurking in the corner of our minds. Judging by the response we get to our prayers I think the Christian God can't be listening all the time. If He didn't hear our prayers, maybe Balor did, and we need all the help we can get.

We have a good number of visitors to the island now that we have sturdy boats to ferry them in and out. The foreigners love to hear us speaking Irish among ourselves but of course we speak English to them, except for our children who aren't old enough to learn English yet and who stare at these people from another world with their strange speech, different faces and fancy clothes. One of the visitors, a powerful clever man who had studied our history, wrote it down for me and the gist of it goes as follows: The island has been occupied for many hundreds of years and we owe our blood to the Nemedians, the Fomorians, then Vikings, then Spaniards from the ill-fated Armada as well as other odds and sods who came here to trade, or to plunder, to convert us, to shelter from bad weather or who were shipwrecked on our shores. Some of these people stayed and married into our native stock.

Nowadays many of our young people go to Scotland to find seasonal work, usually picking potatoes, and some go further and get a building job in England. It sometimes happens that they meet someone over there and get married, but the call of the island is strong and so they often return with their spouses to show them the place which means so much to them. Occasionally the young couple decide to stay here, which is great, for it injects a bit of new blood into the community, but more often than not they return to the bright lights, the big shops, the entertainment, the regular pay-packets, and life in a kinder environment, and you can't blame them. We have a few temporary residents here - the priest, the nurse, the school-teacher and the lighthouse keepers who usually spend just a few years with us then move on, although Fr. Tom has been here for so long, we're beginning to think of him as one of ourselves.

Only two months ago a big electric generator was installed in the village, and that means we have electricity for the first time ever, and there is power and electric light in the pub, the shop, on the pier, in the chapel, the priest's house and the community hall. I suppose it'll get to the lighthouse eventually, but they'll still use paraffin oil for a while yet to make the light that announces our presence in the dark nights to the ships that wander the seas in all weathers. The generator's a bit noisy, but you get used to it, and it doesn't run all night except on special occasions.

It's the 9th August, 1950. The weather is good, the

humour is good and the fishing is good. The last King of the island passed on in April and the three-month mourning period is over, so a new King will be elected shortly. Nothing much out of the ordinary happens here, until recently that is, when a visitor went missing. But this story starts a long way from Inishard, on the far side of the world, in Australia.

CHAPTER ONE

MISSING

Capt. Dan Hilliard called the control tower and having been given permission to land, he nodded to the co-pilot, "Ok Harry, talk to the customers," and turned the Douglas DC 3 onto finals for runway 23 at Adelaide airport after his three-and-a-half-hour flight from Alice Springs.

Most of the twenty-two passengers had been visiting Ayers Rock, or as the Aboriginals called it, Uluru. His friend, business partner and co-pilot Harry Saunders leaned through the open door to the cabin and shouted, "Put your fags out folks, and fasten your seatbelts for landing."

Dan ran his fingers through his dark curly hair, straightened himself in the seat, checked his approach speed, rate of descent, set the flaps, lowered the landing gear, adjusted his sunglasses, and set the twin-engined Dakota gently on the tarmac.

It was July 1950, the second month of Australia's winter

and a comfortable time to sightsee - around 80 degrees Fahrenheit and with about 300 hours of sunshine a month. Dan and Harry had just delivered sixteen people and a load of freight to Alice and were completing the third of their three-times-a-week run between the Springs and Adelaide. The flight took them over mostly un-hospitable desert territory, but the Dakota was a reliable workhorse and had never let them down yet.

Only a few years earlier the same plane had been dropping Allied parachutists into France and Germany, but was now their pride and joy. When the war ended the Dakotas were sold off cheaply and Dan was able to pick one up for a song. He had seen the opportunity to carry freight - medical supplies, engine parts, mail, food, in fact anything and everything that was needed by that isolated community in the middle of the continent. Then he met Harry, an ex-bomber pilot looking for a flying job. The two young men hit it off at once and Harry bought a half share in the plane and they were now a two-man one-plane airline, 'Ghan Air'. There were spare seats kept at both Adelaide and Alice which could be quickly installed in the plane so that any extra space could be given over to passengers.

Many people, mostly tourists, flew back to Adelaide having travelled to Alice on the once-a-week 'Ghan Express' train which took about thirty hours to get there, provided they had a clear run and didn't have to repair sections of track as they went. Sudden, but thankfully infrequent deluges could wash away bits of the rail bed, so a flat truck was hitched immediately behind the engine and carried spare wooden 'sleepers' with which to level up the rails.

The name 'Ghan' came from the camel trains which were the only way to explore the vast interior of the country in the 19th century. The men in charge of the camels were usually from Afghanistan, and the Aussies called them the 'Ghans'. The shortened version stuck.

Dan disembarked his passengers and parked the plane up, leaving Harry to have it re-fuelled and checked out in preparation for the next flight in two days' time. There was a message for him in the Pilot's Office to call with his parents Jack and Susan on his way home. He and his parents lived close to each other in the Lonsdale district in the south of the city. He was a bit weary, but he knew that they wouldn't ask him to call if it wasn't important, so he drove straight to their house.

"Hi dad, hi mum. Any grub for a weary pilot?"

"Come in son. Mum, would you get this lad a bite to eat."

"Bacon and eggs Dan?"

"That'd be great mum. And a big pot of tea, thanks."

His recently retired accountant-father led him through to the dining room and they sat at the table. Dan looked enquiringly at the man who in appearance was just an older version of himself, with dark brown eyes, a weather-beaten lined face and iron-grey hair. Jack was a careful methodical man and Susan was an outdoor adventurous tomboy. He often wondered what attracted them to each other apart from their physical attributes, but whatever it was, it worked. Thirty years later they were still a devoted couple. Dan had inherited his mother's blue eyes and her spirit of adventure, and his sense of caution from his father. Life without risks would be boring as hell, and he took risks, but they were calculated risks.

"What's up dad?"

"It's Richard. Not a dickey bird from him in a month, and he doesn't usually let this amount of time pass without telling us where he is and what his plans are."

"When did you last hear from him?"

"His last letter is dated over a month ago. You know he's writing articles for National Geographic?"

Dan nodded.

"Well, he'd been travelling around the Hebridean islands in Scotland and then going to Ireland, the county of Donegal. I wasn't too worried about not getting a letter from him for a bit, knowing he can be busy, but I got a call today from his editor in National Geographic who wanted to know if we'd heard from him, as he usually sends a report to them every week, and a month had passed without hearing from him. I told him we had no idea either, but if either of us heard something we would contact each other straight away. In his letter Richard said that somebody in Scotland gave him a letter of introduction to a Henry McIlhenny at Glenveagh Castle in Donegal, and that he hoped to stay with him a few days before heading on to his next assignment."

He opened a side-table drawer, took out an envelope and handed it to Dan. "That's the last letter we had."

Dan read the letter a couple of times and marvelled at his brother's great way with words and the stories about his subjects including the little snippets about the interviewees which don't often appear in the finished articles, but which were often the funniest, or rudest, or both. He appeared to be in top form and was looking forward to his sojourns in Donegal. Dan put the letter down and looked into his father's concerned face.

"We're really worried son, what would you advise?"

"I was thinking that letters could get lost in the post, which is possible, but letters to you and National Geographic at the same time? Not likely."

Dan paused, frowning, and slumped down into his seat, thinking it out, then stood up and paced the room for a few moments, making up his mind. "Right, we'll give it one more week to see if we hear anything, and if not, I'll head for

Ireland. I'll use this week to get a replacement pilot to fly with Harry till I get back, and tomorrow I'll telephone this Henry McIlhenny who might know where Richard was heading, and we'll take it from there."

"Would you son? That'd be great. Drink?"

"A beer would be good."

As they drank their beers and chatted about Richard, a shout came from the kitchen, "Grub's up, come and get it."

CHAPTER TWO

CALLING IRELAND

At nine o'clock that night Dan sat in the Pilot's Office at the airport waiting for the call he had booked with a disbelieving operator to 'Churchill 2-5' in Donegal. With the time difference it was only noon in Ireland. Nothing having been heard from his brother in the last week, he was making his travel arrangements and had found Harry a co-pilot to keep 'Ghan Air' up and running. He went over and over all the possibilities of Richard's disappearing off the radar. Accident, possible. Kidnap, why? Maybe in hospital somewhere, possible, but the hospital would have surely been in touch with them if that was the case. Amnesia, possible, but once again someone would have known his identity from his papers and contacted his parents. Letters all lost in the post, most unlikely, but he knew that all this surmising was a pointless exercise.

Richard was no fool. He was careful and methodical, wasn't a heavy drinker, didn't smoke, didn't frequent houses of ill-repute (as far as Dan knew) and normally kept in touch with his family, regaling them with tales of his travels. Richard had no particular girlfriend that he talked about, but had lots of girl-friends as well as men friends, gregarious, yet not ready to settle down. Dan lit up a cigarette and was just putting his cup of coffee to his lips when the phone gave a loud jangle, making him jump and causing him to spill some hot coffee over his hand.

"Damn," he plonked the cup on the desk, grabbed his handkerchief and mopped the spilt coffee and at the same time picked up the receiver with his other hand.

"Hello."

A surprisingly clear Irish female voice said, "Is that the caller for Churchill 2-5?"

"Yes, it is."

"Grand, hold on while I put you through."

A whirring noise was followed by a male voice, "Churchill 2-5."

"Hello, is that Mr. McIlhenny?" asked Dan.

"No, this is his butler Patrick, hold on please and I'll get him for you."

Dan heard the phone being put down and a minute later the handset was picked up and a soft drawling American voice said, "Hallo, who is this?"

"Mr. McIlhenny?"

"Yes."

"My name is Dan Hilliard, and I'm calling from Australia."

"Oh, my deaur, Australia, waal, what can I do for you?"

"I think you might have had my brother Richard Hilliard to stay with you a few weeks ago, is that right?"

"Oh sure, young Richard, a charming boy, he stayed here for a week. He had a letter of introduction from Lord Strathcona in Scotland and..."

"Sorry to interrupt sir, but we may get cut off, so if I could just ask a quick question. Did Richard say where he was going after he left you? We haven't heard from him in five weeks and the family is getting worried about him."

"Let me see, I'm trying to recall if he mentioned it."

Just then the same female voice came on the line, "I know where he went Mr. McIlhenny."

"Is that you Cathleen?"

"Yes Mr. McIlhenny. I just happened to overhear the question from the caller, and I know that Mr. Hilliard went in to Inishard Island on a boat from Bunbeg."

Mr. McIlhenny chuckled, "Well, my deaur, isn't it fortooitus that you happened to be listening in. Thank you, Cathleen."

"Yes indeed, thank you Cathleen," echoed Dan.

"Glad to help," said Cathleen, unabashed, and there was a click at the other end.

"Well, now you have your answer Mr. Hilliard. I sure hope nothing's happened to dear Richard."

"Thank you, sir. If I may ask, where is Inishard?"

"Oh yeah. It's an island off the north west coast of Donegal. I've been there once, a strange place. It's like stepping a hundred years back into the paast."

"I'm very grateful sir, thank you very much and sorry to disturb you."

"Good luck, and if you come to Donegal, you must call me, and..." the line went dead.

Dan put the phone down, lit up another cigarette and pondered this new information. Now we know where he went. Then he smiled and gave thanks again to Cathleen the telephone operator who liked to listen in and jotted the information in his notebook. 'What now?' he wondered, then decided he had better talk to the police in Donegal.

In the main office he found an old well-thumbed world atlas, but there was very little detail on the Ireland map, just the main towns in each county. In the county of Donegal, it showed Letterkenny, Glenties, Killybegs and Donegal, and the closest to the described location of the island of Inishard was Letterkenny, so he got on to enquiries who found the number. He booked a call and returned to the pilot's office to wait. It had been a long day and he closed his eyes. He was just dozing off when the phone jangled and he was put through to the number requested.

"Letterkenny Garda Station."

"Is that the police?"

"Yes, it is."

"Oh good. I'm ringing from Australia looking for my brother Richard Hilliard."

"Can you spell that please?"

"Yes, H-i-l-l-i-a-r-d."

"And you're looking for him?"

"Yes. He was last heard of a few weeks ago when he got a boat out to the island called Inishard, somewhere off your north coast."

"Aye, right sir, I heard something about that. Hold on and I'll put you through to the Superintendent."

There was a silence of nearly a minute, then a soft well-spoken voice said, "Superintendent Ginty speaking, may I have your name please?"

"Yes sir, my name is Dan Hilliard and I'm making enquiries about my brother Richard who went to Inishard island a few weeks ago, and we haven't heard from him since. The constable said that he had heard the name and that you may be able to help."

"Well, Mr. Hilliard, I do know of your brother. Normally we don't discuss open cases over the phone, but as you're calling from Australia, I understand your concern, and I need information from you. What we do know is that Richard Hilliard did go to Inishard and was there for a number of days before being reported missing. We sent a team out to the island and they searched it and talked to everybody, but we came up with nothing. He just disappeared."

"Do you suspect foul play Superintendent, or could he have left the island without anyone knowing?"

There was a silence during which Dan's heart sank into his boots, then the Superintendent said, "It doesn't look good Mr. Hilliard. As far as we can ascertain, no boats left the island with him on board and if he did leave on a boat, why would he have left his suitcase behind in his digs. He must have kept his personal documents on him as all we could find in his room were some clothes, a pair of shoes, toilet things and big notebooks with descriptions of various places in Scotland, but nothing that gave us his address. There doesn't appear to be any, or at least enough reason for anyone to harm him. He was at a ceili, a dance, the night before he disappeared. Now, there may have been drink taken, and if he fell into the sea a body has not yet been found. So, until that happens, if it happens, there is nothing more we can do. I am sorry."

Dan's heart sank further as he listened to the slightly distorted voice from half a world away. There wasn't anything in that voice that gave him cause for hope.

"We have his small suitcase with his bits and pieces here at the station. What would you want me to do with them?"

"Would you hold them for me Mr. Ginty, I'm planning to come to Ireland and I'll collect them at some stage."

"Aye, that'll do. We'll keep them for you here. Now, if I could have your address and telephone number in Australia please. Would you be the next of kin?"

"That would be my parents," and Dan gave the policeman their details, but asked that he be allowed to break the news of Richard's disappearance to them. Superintendent Ginty thought that that was a good idea.

“Thank you, Superintendent. Thank you very much. Bye for now.”

An upset Dan slowly placed the receiver back on its cradle and a sudden fear came on him that he would probably never see his brother again. He thought of all their happy times together and visualised Richard’s big smile as he patiently showed his younger brother how to make camp in the ‘bush’, how to light a fire using just sticks, how to throw a boomerang. Suddenly Dan sobbed bitter tears at the thought of life without Richard.

After a few minutes, he washed his face, composed himself and returned to his parent’s house where he recounted the story of the phone call to Henry McIlhenny but not the one to the police.

“What do we do now?” asked his mother, “we’ve got to do something I think.”

Both parents looked at Dan expectantly.

“You’re right mum, It’s all organised. I’m heading for Ireland.”

CHAPTER THREE

DAN ARRIVES IN INISHARD

A week later Dan was crouched down, wearing borrowed oilskins, his back against the gunwale of a forty-foot half-decker fishing boat trying to keep as dry as possible, as the spray from a choppy sea and a headwind drenched the occupants with every downward plunge into a trough. A young couple and their two children had some shelter under the small forward covered deck which contained and smelled of diesel oil, fishing nets and damp rope. He was Alex somebody or other, a returning islander, with an English wife and kids who looked as if they had been dropped into the middle of a horror film. Alex was kept busy handing out paper bags to his non-seafaring wife and kids who were pale, and were using the sick-bags for their designated purpose.

The other three men on board were islanders, one puffing contentedly on a pipe and wrestling with the long arm of the rudder, as the water ran down his full-bodied oilskins and wellington boots. The men all wore flat caps, and chatted away in Irish, except when Dan asked a question. Then their musical accents and the placements of the words indicated that they were translating directly from the Irish. As he did when flying over the 'Dead Heart' of Australia, he kept an attentive ear to the engine and hoped that this one wouldn't fail just now. It seemed to rumble and whine away happily enough, and the relaxed chat of the men reassured him that there was nothing to worry about.

He was feeling a bit queasy himself, but that had only started as he watched the others being sick into their bags, so he turned around and looked back towards the receding mainland. The mid-section on the boat had barrels of beer and Guinness, spirits, foodstuffs and whatever else had been requested by the islanders, all snugly tied down under a tarpaulin. Bags of coal and logs were stacked against the tarpaulin on the top of which lay an old bicycle and a rather wet miserable-looking black and white collie dog.

He had wondered how best to approach the search for his brother, and had decided that he would go incognito at first and ask questions in a roundabout way to see what he could uncover. Knowing that he was related to the missing man might inhibit the flow of information or even gossip, all of which could be helpful. So, he had booked his seat on the boat as 'Dan Livingstone' and given himself a new career as a botanist so that he could wander around the whole island pretending to examine the flora while keeping his eyes and ears open.

With half an hour to go to the island, the wind dropped and the sea lessened, making the trip more comfortable, and when they came into the lee of Inishard it was comparatively placid. The little family perked up and came out from under the forward cabin to look at the approaching island, the father pointing out things to his wife and children, and they and Dan were grateful for a tin mug of sweet tea poured from a large thermos flask produced by the skipper. Dan scanned the island and thought of his brother seeing the same panorama – the well-sheltered pier and behind it a good number of white-painted houses and a couple of larger buildings, all with small windows outlined in blue, red, yellow or green, their doors matching their windows. The sun came out and the whole place looked peaceful and welcoming, and he and the others, he was certain, were looking forward to being off the boat and ashore. The land sloped up quite steeply behind the village to considerable cliffs overlooking the open Atlantic Ocean.

The half-decker came alongside the pier and tied up.

CHAPTER FOUR

GLEESON'S PUB

Paddy Gleeson, the owner of the pub at the head of the pier watched the half-decker tie up and knew that his pub would be the first stop for the new arrivals. He was right. Several locals were sitting at the bar with pints in front of them when the door opened and the crew of the half-decker and their passengers walked in, the young couple with two children and a man on his own who looked to be somewhere in his mid to late twenties. This man ordered a pint of Guinness from the smiling girl behind the bar and took it to a table overlooking the harbour.

Paddy suddenly recognised the father of the family who were huddling around the big coal fire and greeted him loudly in Irish, "Jeez, is that you Alex Dougan?"

"It is indeed Paddy and you knew me, and me away for the last eight years."

"Well, well, well, eight years is it eh? Sure, I'd know you if you were half-burnt. And now you're a married man with wanes. Does your wife speak the Irish?"

"I'm afraid not," admitted Alex.

"Righto then, we'll speak the English for the benefit of herself and the wanes. Now, introduce me."

"Veronica, this is Paddy Gleeson, the biggest chancer between here and Boston."

He ruffled the children's hair. "This is Liam and Eithne."

"I'm very pleased to meet you Mr. Gleeson," said Veronica politely.

"It's Paddy. Mr. Gleeson my late lamented father died years ago, God rest his soul. You're looking a bit green about the gills Veronica. It was a bit rough out there, so what you need is a brandy and port, maybe an orange for the wanes and a pint for you Alex?"

They smiled their assent and he went to the bar and gave the order to his daughter, Bella, and carried the drinks back to their table.

Veronica thanked him. "Alex has told me so much about Inishard and you in particular, that I feel I know you already."

"Oh jeez, now that is worrying. Anyway, changing the subject quickly, is it just the two wanes you have?"

"No indeed," said Alex "We have three younger ones behind in England."

Paddy's eyes widened. "How long are you staying?"

"We go home the middle of September, then it's back to work in the tunnels for McAlpines. I've spent so much of me life underground I feel like a rabbit."

Paddy laughed, "With five wanes in eight years I doubt there's a bit of the rabbit about ye alright."

Paddy and Alex laughed at the joke. Veronica blushed.

Paddy changed tack, "Who's yer man came over on the boat with ye?"

Alex looked at Dan and wrinkled his brow, thinking, "He's called...ah...ah... what did he say his name was Veronica?"

"Livingstone, Dan Livingstone."

"Aye, now I remember. He's here from some college or other to study the plants on the island."

At that point two of Alex's old friends came over to shake his hand and Alex exclaimed, "John-Joe and Anton, yiz haven't changed a day, and is that Peter I see, all growed up, and that couldn't be wee Bella, my God it is."

Paddy excused himself from the company and going over to Dan's table, coughed lightly to attract his attention as Dan was staring out at the ocean. As he turned around, Paddy said with a serious face, "Dr. Livingstone, I presume. If it's the source of the Nile you're looking for, you shoulda turned left in Bunbeg."

He laughed at his own joke and Dan couldn't help smiling broadly, and immediately took a liking to this man. Paddy stretched out his hand which Dan stood up and clasped.

"You're very welcome, sir to Inishard. I'm Paddy Gleeson, the proprietor of Gleeson's Bar, the best pub on the island, the only pub on the island. Now, if I can help you enjoy your stay with us in any way, just let me know."

"Thank you very much Mr. Gleeson."

"Paddy please, Paddy. There's no formality here."

"In that case you had better call me Dan."

Paddy taking encouragement from the friendly interaction and determined to find out more, pulled up a chair and sat at the table with Dan, "Is this your first visit to Inishard Dan? I thought I'd seen you somewhere before."

Dan's heart leapt and he wondered if they would see the similarity between himself and Richard, even though Richard was slimmer, two years older, not quite as tall as Dan, and had brown eyes.

"No sir, sorry, I mean Paddy. It's my first time in this part of the world. The family came from Belfast originally but emigrated to Australia when I was a kid. I've been teaching botany at the University of Adelaide in south Australia for a few years now."

"Is that so. And what brings you to this distant outpost of the Empire?"

Dan was glad that he had done a little research to back up his fake story and he was quite impressed with the references made by Gleeson to 'Livingstone and the Nile' and 'outpost of the Empire'. He cautioned himself to tread carefully as he replied, "I was reading up on the unique plants of the islands off the west coast of Ireland, and I decided to come and see them for myself and collect some examples. I'll be spending some time on Tory, Gola, Owey and Arranmore as well as here." He laughed. "If I discover a new variety, they might name it after me. How 'bout that, eh?"

"Begod, aren't ye the great man, comin' all this way to look at our weeds. Are ye staying long?"

"A couple of weeks at most should do me here, and that reminds me, is there anywhere I can stay? I tried ringing in advance, but they told me the line was down, so I just took pot luck and came anyway."

At that Paddy turned around to the bar, "Peter, c'mere a minute."

Peter came slowly forward and Dan saw that he was probably in his late teens, looked like he wasn't the brightest star in the firmament, and seemed very shy.

"Run over to Keenans and see if they have a room for one man for two weeks. Now remember that, one man, one room, two weeks," said Paddy.

Peter repeated the order in a slow hesitant voice and a stammer, and then hurried out of the pub. Paddy went over to the bar and pulled two pints of Guinness and brought them back to Dan's table. Dan reached for his wallet but

Paddy put his hand out and stopped him. "This one's on the house and the other's for me," they toasted one another, "Sláinte, Good Health," and took long draughts.

"Paddy, when I was reading up about the islands, it seems that in summer it's all fishing, farming and gathering seaweed for fertilizer and so on, but I was wondering how you spend the long winter nights and maybe you cut off from contact with the outside world. What do you do to kill the time?"

"Well now, young Dan, two things. Inishard is part of Donegal, so we just call over there the 'mainland'. Which reminds me, one of the kids in our school writing a composition about our geography said 'Ireland is an island off Inishard'," he laughed heartily, Dan shaking his head and smiling at the perception of the world through a child's eyes.

"As regards your question, we're never lost for something to do here. We have our wirelesses to give us music and stories and plays and news from Radio Eireann in Dublin, or the BBC in Belfast, but it has its drawbacks. The battery can run out in the middle of somethin' interesting. But mostly we do what people on islands have done for centuries. We gather here in the pub or in somebody's kitchen where we sing, we play accordions, fiddles and penny whistles, we tell yarns, and lies, and ghost stories and after a few bottles of homemade central heatin' we dance the old dances on the flag floors till the wee hours. The young men use these occasions to show off to the lassies and if they get a chance to walk them home..." Paddy tapped the side of his nose. "Do you follow me?" he nudged Dan and laughed, his merry eyes twinkling.

"Yes, Paddy," grinned Dan, "I follow you."

Bella had been watching the exchanges between her father and Dan with some interest. He was the most handsome thing she had ever seen, like he just stepped out of her film magazines, and she wondered if he was available. She was not yet twenty, chubby, cheerful, nice eyes, and her white blouse struggled to conceal a generous bosom, which meant that the male customers preferred the bar stools to the tables. She looked at her reflection in a mirrored advertisement for Guinness, fluffed her dyed-blonde hair and checked her make-up, which she didn't really need as she was a pretty girl. However, all the film stars in 'Motion Picture Story' wore make-up. She kicked off her father's old slippers and slid her feet into her high heels, tucked the blouse into her flowery skirt causing every male eye at the bar to swivel in her direction, and wandered over to Dan's table supposedly to pick up empty glasses, but really to get an introduction to the 'dreamboat' whom she reckoned on closer inspection looked like a cross between Clark Gable and John Derek.

"Hello."

Dan stood up, "Hello to you."

Bella looked pointedly at her father who got the message.

"Oh Dan, this is my daughter Bella. Bella, this is Mr. Livingstone, from Australia."

"Pleased to meet you, Mr. Livingstone," purred Bella in her best sexy voice.

"Glad to meet you Bella, please call me Dan." He offered his hand which she took and held on to.

"Do you need a place to stay Dan? We have a spare room."

Paddy interrupted, "Aw shhhag," and slapped his hand to his head. "I shoulda' thought of that meself, I must be gettin' old. I've sent Peter over to Keenans to book Dan in, but if they can't take him then we'll get the room ready."

"Will I get the room ready, just in case?" she asked her father hoping against hope that the Keenans couldn't take him.

"Naw, we'd better wait and see, now back to the bar with you, you'll have plenty of time to chat with Dan. He's goin' to be here for a couple of weeks."

"Oh, that's nice. See you later, Dan," she stepped lightly

back to the bar, her head in the clouds, seeing visions of herself and Dan falling in love and walking up the aisle together, or even running away to Gretna Green to get married in the old forge. Her reverie was shattered by a voice from the bar counter, "Jeez Bella, for the third time, would ye fill 'er up again," an empty pint glass was pushed in her direction. Back to reality.

Paddy looked at Dan and shook his head. "Well, it looks like you have an admirer already Dan, and she doesn't mind showin' it. Not at all like the old days, when a girl would rather be crucified than give the slightest hint that she was interested in a particular man. Ah don't know what the world's comin' to, young wans nowadays, tch tch tch. And they can't cook anymore either, d'ye know, she made a cake last week, and honest to God, it woulda' sunk a duck. Ah, here's Peter back, can they take Mr. Livingstone Peter?"

"Y-y-yes they can Mr. Gleeson."

"Right then Dan, Peter here'll show you the way and we'll see you later."

Dan, still laughing inwardly at the mental image of drowning ducks full of Bella's cake, shook hands with Paddy. "Thanks for everything Paddy."

Peter picked up the suitcase and followed by Dan headed for the door past a love-struck Bella. Dan gave her a nod and a smile and followed Peter out the door.

CHAPTER FIVE

DAN CHECKS IN

As they walked through the village on a dirt road with open water drains bordered by slabs of stone on either side, Dan remembered what Henry McIlhenny had said about it being like something from a hundred years earlier, and he was beginning to agree. There were a few dogs trotting around and an occasional person standing at their front door who nodded to him as he and Peter passed. He spotted a few donkeys grazing behind the cottages, a couple of decrepit tractors which looked like they had been there for years and would never belch smoke again, and a few old bicycles. Three or four un-lived-in houses spoiled the overall pleasing look of the whitewashed cottages, and there were no motor cars to be seen.

"Peter?"

"Y-yes Mr. Liv-ing-stone"

"Are you doing anything tomorrow morning?"

"N-no Mr. Liv-ing-stone, I'm n-not, b-b-but I have to w-work in the p-pub l-later on."

"Would you be able to show me around the island after breakfast?"

Peter dropped his head. He had barely ever spoken to a visitor before and was nervous and shy. "I'm n-not sure Mr. Liv-ing-stone."

"Oh, please Peter. I need a friend to show me around and I'll be happy to pay you."

Peter was amazed. This big good-looking man wanted him to be his friend, him! "D-don't want m-money Mr. Liv-ing-stone. I'll do it f-for you, f-for nothin'."

"That's very kind Peter, thanks so much. So now that we're friends, my name is Dan."

"Dan," he smiled "t-that's e-e-easier than Mr. Liv-ing-stone. This is K-Keenans."

"See you here at ten in the morning then?"

Peter nodded.

"Thanks Peter."

They solemnly shook hands and Peter turned away with a big smile on his face and trotted back to the pub to tell Bella about his friend Dan.

John and Kathleen Keenan were a gentle quiet-spoken couple who opened their house to visitors after their three children grew up and left the island. A 'settle' sat near the fireplace, a wooden bench seat with arms and a back, but John Keenan proudly demonstrated that it could be opened out into a bed at night. "But we don't use it anymore - only if the house is full."

In the ingle nook stood a crane with hanging-hooks for holding cooking pots. For the first time Dan smelled the pleasant odour of burning peat. One easy-chair and one rocking chair sat on either side of the fire. A sturdy looking mantlepiece held some framed photographs of children and grand-children and two Staffordshire China dogs sat smiling at each other from either end of the mantelpiece. Below the window which overlooked the street there was a wooden table which was covered in flowered oilcloth on which sat a battery-powered radio and a vase with paper flowers.

Tucked in under the table were four chairs, and on the wall-papered walls were four sepia photographic portraits of stern looking men and women, their parents Dan was told, a picture of the 'Sacred Heart of Jesus' and beside it a framed photograph of a man he later found out was the President of Ireland, Sean T. O'Kelly. A cupboard held shining dishes and the drawers below held all other dining requirements. A wag-at-the-wall clock completed the inventory apart from the small dish of holy water which was screwed onto the inside door frame.

After a cup of tea and two delicious home-made scones with strawberry jam, Kathleen led Dan up a narrow staircase to show him his room. It comprised a single bed covered in a patchwork quilt, a chair and table which held an oil lamp, and against another wall on a long wide shelf, a delft wash-basin sat firmly a circular hole in the wood, and beside it sat a large jug of water, a bar of soap and a towel and a wooden-framed tilting mirror for shaving. The small window in the back wall looked out over the land towards the cliffs.

Dan was about to ask about toilet facilities when he spotted the handle of a chamber pot sticking out from under the bed. 'Oh my God,' he thought, 'how am I going to manage here'?

Mrs. Keenan saw him frowning and staring at the object under the bed and she laughed,

"Ah dear Mr. Livingstone, I forgot to say we have a proper

toilet at the back of the house. That yoke is just for emergencies."

"Whew, that's a relief anyway," laughed Dan and gazed around the room.

"I hope it suits you alright?" Kathleen asked anxiously.

"It's perfect," said Dan.

"Oh good. There's a hot-water bottle in your bed just now, and I'll freshen it up later."

"Mrs. Keenan?"

"Kathleen."

"Ok then, Kathleen. I'm Dan. I've had a very long journey and I'm going to visit your facilities and then I'm going to crash."

"Crash?"

"Go to bed and sleep the sleep of the just."

"But it's only seven o'clock."

"That I know."

"Ok then, what time will you want breakfast?"

"Whatever time suits you, Kathleen. I plan to have a relaxing time while I'm here."

"That's grand, we'll say nine then. Bacon and eggs ok?"

"Has my mother been in touch with you?"

She did a double take.

"Just joking, it's my favourite, Kathleen."

"You're from Australia then?"

"I am indeed."

"Well, isn't that a coincidence. We had an Australian man staying here not long ago, maybe you knew him? A Richard Hilliard."

Dan's heart jumped at the mention of his brother, but he managed to give a laugh and said, "Australia's a big place Kathleen."

"Of course, of course. Silly of me. I just thought. Never mind. Well off you go and we'll see you in the morning."

. . .

Dan visited the 'facility' a narrow little shed, but spotlessly clean and fresh-smelling, then returned to the house, said his goodnights, and climbed up to his room where he washed his face, cleaned his teeth, climbed into bed and lay for a long time, his brain whirling at the fact that Richard stayed in this very house, possibly in this room, in this bed. He suddenly felt very close to his brother and as a tear trickled down his cheek, he wondered what he might find out, hoping that there would be a happy ending to his quest. He hugged his hot-water bottle and it wasn't long before fatigue won the day and he leaned over and blew out the oil lamp.

CHAPTER SIX

DAN GOES EXPLORING AND MEETS SIOBHAN

Dan woke up at five thirty and couldn't get back to sleep so he got up, dressed, descended the steep stairs quietly and left the house. It was a lovely morning, the sun just beginning to appear and no one awake it seemed, except himself. The fishing boats were tied up alongside each other at the pier and on such a day must surely be heading out. The gulls sat patiently on the pier wall waiting on the fishermen to arrive, as they had the chance of a free breakfast when nets were shaken out and decks were cleared before departure.

He strolled along the shore towards the south of the island, listening to the piping of the oyster-catchers as they busily foraged the shoreline stabbing the shallows with their bright orange beaks. He sat down and listened to the gurgling watery clink of pebbles being dropped by the last small breaking wave and smelled the kelp lying on the shoreline where it had been left by the last tide. The light was clear and wonderful, the air was exhilarating. This was a wonderful place, and Dan felt that having one day like this could make up for a week of lashing gales and rough seas, and that one day was probably the reason that the Island was still populated. He heard the half-deckers start up and the screams of the gulls in the distance and a while later saw the boats round the point as they dispersed in different directions to trawl for herring and mackerel.

Dan was quite sure that the Keenans wouldn't be looking through his belongings when he was out, but just in case he locked the briefcase which contained his traveller's cheques, the bulk of his cash and passport and put the briefcase inside his suitcase.

John and Kathleen smiled a welcome as he clattered down the narrow staircase for breakfast. They were surprised to know that he had been up and out hours ago. They talked about the beautiful day it was, and shared other weather-related stories as he tucked into a large plate of well-fried bacon, fried homemade soda bread, fried tomatoes and two eggs and the pot of tea. He thought that this tea was the best ever, and wondered why. Maybe it was the softness of the water, or the peat-smoke, but anyway, whatever it was, it was fantastic.

The Keenans taught him a few words of Irish. Más á do thoil á, please. Slán, goodbye. Fáilte, welcome. Dia is Mhuire duit, a rather long way of saying hello he thought. They explained that it meant 'God and Mary to you', but 'Dia duit' would do. He kept repeating them until they were reasonably happy with his pronunciation.

He threw his small ex-army knapsack over his shoulder and at ten to ten he stepped outside to see Peter sitting on the front wall waiting. "Dia is Mhuire duit," boomed Dan confidently as he opened the little gate to the street.

Peter laughed and responded in Irish but when Dan just stood and stared uncomprehendingly Peter said, "Hello D-dan."

"Hiya Peter. Well, shall we go?"

Peter nodded.

"Why don't we go up towards the lighthouse first."

"Ok," said Peter and started up the road out of the village. Peter was carrying a brown paper bag. Dan chastised himself, 'Damn, I should have brought a box or something suitable for my botanical samples'.

"Where's the shop Peter?"

Peter pointed to a house a few doors further on which had the word 'Siopa' written on a card in the window. The shop sold everything from rubber boots to frying pans and also doubled up as a Post Office. A sharp-featured, thin, middle-aged lady wearing pink-framed glasses appeared from the back of the shop as the doorbell tinkled when he entered.

"Good morning, Mr. Livingstone."

"Good morning, Miss?" responded Dan, taken aback that his name was known already. But then, it was a small place and visitors were a novelty.

"Rodgers, Mary Rodgers, Mrs. Mary Rodgers. Mary will do."

"Well then, good morning, Mary. Could I have two bottles of orange, twenty cigarettes, any brand will do, a bag of mixed sweets and a packet of those biscuits. I also need something to put plants in, my sample case and I had a parting of the ways somewhere between Adelaide and Dublin."

As Mary searched the shelves for an appropriate receptacle she remarked, "Yes I hear you are a botanist from Australia. That's interesting. Long way away Australia, isn't it? Would this do?" she offered him an empty biscuit tin.

"Thanks Mary, it'll do very well." He put his purchases into the tin, the tin into the knapsack, and paid the lady.

"Is that Peter I see outside?"

"Yep, he's showing me the island."

"Mmmm," she sniffed "I hope he's some use to you."

"Oh, I'm sure he will be. Thanks, see you later."

Dan had a book of Native Irish Plants with him, and every so often on their walk he would stop to examine the small flowers and plants and consult the book as to their identity. Nothing large grew here because of the climate and the poverty of the soil. He surprised himself that he was starting to enjoy finding and identifying the different species. The two men talked as they wandered along.

"Have you been off the island Peter?"

"Yeh. I was in L-Letterkenny once, in the h-hospital when I was sick."

"Is that the furthest you've been?"

"Yeh."

"Have you any brothers and sisters?"

"Naw."

"Have you a mother and father?"

"Naw, not a r-real m-mammy and daddy."

"What do you mean Peter?"

"God was m-my father and M-Mary was my mother. The p-priest told me that. G-God left me at Father Tom's d-door when I was a b-babby. Now the p-priest is my n-new father and M-Madge is my new m-mother."

"Well, isn't that interesting. Who is Madge, Peter?"

"She w-works in Father Tom's house."

"And you live with them?"

"Yeh."

Dan wondered at the background to that story, but no

doubt he would hear later. They walked to the big gates of the Lighthouse on the most northerly point of the island, but didn't see anyone about, so they turned right and walked up the sloping rocky ground to the cliffs. The cliffs were magnificent, dropping two or three hundred feet almost straight down to the gun-metal sea which rumbled and crashed below them. There were two curraghs, two men in each, which looked like toys bobbing around on the swell close to the cliffs and Peter told him they were lobster fishing. Dan looked back down the full length of the island, and spotted a man on a bicycle heading up to the lighthouse from the village. 'The Keeper must have been shopping' he mused.

He and Peter sat down and enjoyed the warmth, the many rabbits hopping in and out of their burrows, the sound of the sea below, Iceland straight north from here and Canada and the USA due west. It was remote but a different remoteness to the one he was used to. This one was gentle compared to the tans, beiges, browns and dark ochres of the 'Dead Heart' of Australia and the searing heat from a pale blue cloudless sky. He lay quietly, eyes closed, enjoying the gentle heat of the sun and the various scents of the island carried on the ozone-rich air.

"Dan, Dan!"

He opened his eyes, startled, and saw Peter standing over him holding a bunch of greenery.

"I p-picked these f-for you Dan."

Dan blinked and realised that he had fallen asleep. His body clock wasn't used to being this far from home yet.

"Great, thanks a lot Peter, now let's have something to eat," he opened the tin and handed Peter a bottle of orange and some biscuits. They finished off with some sweets and Dan lit a cigarette and then offered Peter one which he declined.

"Don't s-smoke."

"Very wise Peter, it's a bad habit."

"Want to s-see what I have?"

"Sure thing. What have you got?"

Peter opened his paper bag and took out a wooden aeroplane, rough but a pretty good likeness, and he waved it around making engine noises.

"Hey, that's terrific Peter, did you make that yourself?"

"Yeh," Peter smiled hugely.

"May is see it?"

"Yeh."

"It's very good. You have the propellor and the windows in as well. Did you ever see a real plane?"

"Naw. I saw p-pictures in a b-book and I s-saw them away up in the air flyin' a-above the island goin' to America and b-back again."

"Peter, do you know where Australia is?"

"I t-think s-so. It's away past Letterkenny anyway."

"Well, it's thousands of miles from here, and I spent three days in aeroplanes just to get here."

Peter looked at him disbelievingly.

Dan smiled, "I did, really. Do you know a plane can fly at two hundred miles an hour, and there are lots of people in it, and pretty ladies bring you a cup of tea and food to eat?"

Peter laughed out loud. "C-can you drink tea at two h-hundred m-miles an hour?"

"Sure, you can."

Peter was convinced that Dan was joking and he laughed merrily and mimed trying to drink tea at two hundred miles an hour, running around waving a pretend cup, spilling it all over himself and peering into the empty cup. Dan was delighted to see the young man relaxing in his company, and he and Peter were so engrossed in their mirth that they didn't see a figure approach them. As she got closer, Peter spotted her and ran to meet her.

"Vonnie, Vonnie!"

"Hello Peter, what are you doing?"

"D-drinking tea at two hundred m-miles an hour," he giggled and took her by the hand.

"C-come and see Dan, my f-friend."

Dan got to his feet as they approached and saw a most attractive girl with auburn hair tied back in a pony-tail. She was smiling, lovely teeth he noted, as well as a fine athletic figure. Mid-twenties, he thought. She was wearing blue shorts which showed off shapely sun-tanned legs, a dark blue sweater and sandals.

"Dan, this is m-my friend Vonnie."

"Hello Vonnie, Dan Livingstone."

They shook hands.

"Hello Dan. Nice to meet you. Perhaps I should point out that Peter is the only one who calls me Vonnie. My name is Siobhan but Peter finds Vonnie easier to say."

She had a voice like warm honey and he realised that this was no ordinary island girl. This was an educated young woman.

"Will you sit down?"

"Thank you."

Peter went back to playing with his plane, and Dan offered Siobhan a cigarette which she declined and as he was lighting one for himself, she said, "I understand you're originally from Belfast, now living in Adelaide, teaching botany at the University, you're here for two weeks to study our island flora, you're fond of a pint of Guinness and Bella Gleeson has set her cap at you."

Dan had been staring open-mouthed at her forgetting he had a lit match in his hand until he felt the sting and threw it from him. "Ow, damn. Sorry Von, Siobhan, but how?"

She gave a tinkling laugh, and he noticed that she had hazel eyes.

"Primitive we may be on this island, but our news-gathering system is second to none."

He shook his head wonderingly. "I've never seen better. May I be so bold as to ask who Siobhan is?"

"Siobhan Gray, school-teacher to the present generation of Inishardian children. The school is closed for the summer, but I decided to stay on. I have two years of a three-year contract completed. My grandparents came from here, hence a genetic desire to work here, if only for a while. My family lives in Falcarragh now and before I came here, I taught in Dublin and London. Is that enough to be going on with?"

"Do you realise it would have taken two English people a week of embarrassed indirect questioning to find out that much about each other?"

They smiled at each other and she agreed with him, her heart thumping. God he was handsome, and he seemed nice as well. 'C'mon girl' she cautioned herself, 'control yourself, you're a respectable school-teacher, now go, before you give yourself away'.

She stood up, "Well, Dan, it was nice to meet you."

He stood up as well, disappointed. "Do you have to go?"

"I'm afraid so."

"Just one more question."

"Yes?"

"Did you say 'Miss' Siobhan Gray?"

"I didn't say, but it is 'Miss'."

Dan just smiled, as did she, pleased that he had asked the question, and he that she was not married.

"How's the botany business going? Have you found any Oncidium yet? There's a lot of it up here on the cliffs."

"Er no, not yet. I heard it was to be found here alright. Can we talk again, soon?"

She looked puzzled but only momentarily. "If you like. I share a small house on the edge of the village with Grace

Johnston the nurse and I give her a hand when she's busy, which isn't often. I expect you'll be going to the dance in the hall on Friday, so I'll see you there. By the way, in case you haven't heard, the dances don't start here until about midnight and end just before breakfast. And you're here at a very important time too as a new King of Inishard will be elected that night as well."

They shook hands again, and Dan suggested that Peter might go back with her as it appeared he had work in the pub each afternoon.

"Of course, come on Peter."

Peter looked anxiously at Dan who thanked him and told him to go back with Vonnie, and he would see him again soon.

Dan sat and watched the two figures receding into the distance, and for the first time in his life he felt that watching her go was like losing part of himself. It was very strange. He had other girlfriends but none of them had affected him like this one. He felt quite bewildered at the huge impact the brief meeting had made on him. He was amazed to find that as he lit a cigarette his hands were trembling slightly, and he stared at them.

Siobhan must have met Richard, surely, and would be able to tell him something about his brother if anyone could. He lay back on the grass and thought about Siobhan Gray, a vision of beauty on a remote island off a remote part of Ireland, and the lines of a poem he had learned at school came into his head, 'Full many a flower is born to blush unseen and waste it's sweetness on the desert air'. He smiled as he remembered the line from the elegy by Thomas Gray. Well, Mr. Gray, this flower, who happens to share your surname, has been seen, and if I have anything to do with it, she won't waste her sweetness on the desert air. He realised guiltily that thoughts of Siobhan had filled his mind and he mentally apologised to Richard for momentarily losing sight of his mission. 'I'll speak to Siobhan at the next opportunity' he promised him.

CHAPTER SEVEN

THE PUB GETS RAIDED

Gleeson's Bar was packed. Men were sitting at the counter and at the tables, and not a drink in front of any of them. They murmured among themselves and cast anxious glances at the clock behind the bar. It was 3.45p.m. Paddy and Bella were polishing glasses. Paddy put down his cloth and announced loudly to the dejected assembly, "Come on now lads, yiz know the law. Yiz'll just have to wait till four o'clock when the 'holy hour' is over. Maybe yiz would like a drink while you're waitin'?"

There was laughter and applause and Paddy and Bella were flat out pulling pints and pouring shorts which the patrons were just getting tucked into when the bar door crashed open and Jack Shaughnessy the lighthouse keeper appeared in the doorway gasping for breath.

"Quick Paddy, the Guards is here on a raid. They're just

comin' to the pier now. I'd of been here quicker but me bike punctured and I had to run most of the way."

"Good man Jack. I owe you one. Right lads, town meetin'. You know the drill, finish the drinks quick, get rid of the bottles. Bella hide the poitín in the usual place."

In ninety seconds flat there was a meeting of the villagers sitting on two lines of chairs being addressed by Paddy.

"Now, as yiz know lads, I have written again to the County Council to complain about the fact that our dole..."

The door crashed open again as three members of the Garda Siochana rushed in with the Sergeant shouting, "Gotcha Gleeson, nobody move." They stopped dead and looked at the sober gentlemen of the village staring at them.

The Gardaí looked bewildered in the silence which ensued, until Paddy spoke. "Is it yourself Sergeant Flanagan. What a pleasant surprise, but as you can see, we're havin' a town meetin', so I'll have to ask you to wait outside until we wind up the meeting. I would offer you a drink, but as you can see it's not four o'clock yet."

The Sergeant huffed and puffed having been made to look foolish, and he bellowed, "Now look, see here Gleeson, don't you try to be smart with me. We're here on official business, and we can enter were we like, when we like, if we suspect there is poitín on the premises, or the liquor licensing laws is bein' broke in any way, any way mind you."

"Poitín in my pub Sergeant, never! Sure, there's no poitín made on this island at all at all. What makes you think there is?"

The Sergeant smiled, a cat about to play with a mouse. "We have it on good authority from various inebriated persons apprehended on the mainland, that the source of their fall from grace was made on this island, and dispensed on this premises, so it is beholden on me, the guardian of law and order to follow up on this information and bring the distillator and the distributor of this illicit drink to face the full fury of the law."

"Sure, Sergeant dear, if they were drunk when you questioned them, they wouldn't know one island from the other. They probably got it from the Tory men. Them boyo's is up to everythin'. Anyway, it's four o'clock lads, so we'll finish the meetin' the morra. Now Sergeant Flanagan, it would be my pleasure to offer you and your two stalwart companions a little sustenance after your protracted and uncomfortable journey from the mainland. I seem to remember that a Napoleon brandy was your choice on your last visit."

"Shhh! keep your voice down man," muttered the Sergeant, and clutching his substantial belly he whispered, "Well, now that you mention it, I do feel a wee bit queasy, the oul' stomach y'know, never a good sailor, so I'll just have a large brandy and port to settle me stomach."

Paddy turned and addressed the two young Gardaí, noticing that Bella and Peter were once again behind the bar having hidden the bottles of poitín under the floorboards in the kitchen.

"And yourselves, gentlemen, what can I get you?"

The guards didn't hear him as they were casting lover-boy glances at Bella who was giving them flirty returns.

He addressed them again louder and got their attention, "Gentlemen, the young lady whose details you are committing to memory is my daughter Bella and she would be happy to pour you a drink if Mr. Flanagan says it's ok. What about it Sergeant?"

"Aye alright, you boys deserve one as I observe that it hasn't affected your dedication to studying a possible law-breaker, so as a reward ye can have a drink. By the way Paddy, this is Garda Staunton and that's Garda Maguire. It's their first time here."

"Pleased to make your acquaintance gentlemen, so what'll it be?"

"The same as the sergeant, thanks."

"Haven't yiz the fine simple tastes," muttered Paddy with a sinking heart. "Have a seat men and Bella will bring them over to you. Bella, would you bring these three guardians of the law three large brandies and port. How long is it now Sergeant since your last visit and when can we expect the pleasure of your company again?"

The Sergeant laughed derisively, "These are surprise raids Gleeson, you didn't expect me to fall for that one now did ye?"

Paddy laughed too but groaned inwardly as he saw Bella emptying about a quarter of a bottle of brandy into three glasses. "Ah there's no way to catch you out Sergeant. You weren't behind the door when they were handin' out the brains."

The young Guards found it hard to drag their eyes away from Bella who basked in their attention and smiled and laughed with the other customers while casting sidelong looks at them, particularly at Garda Staunton, the more handsome of the two.

She wondered what it would be like to be a Garda's wife. It was a good job with a pension and she would see different parts of the country. 'I could do worse', she thought, 'and if I can't get the lovely Dan, then I could do worse than catch Guard Staunton. I must find out his first name before he leaves. Aw Christ, I hope he's not married. Naw, I don't think so. He looks too innocent'.

As the three Gardaí were finishing off their drinks and thinking they were about to leave, Paddy said, "Sergeant Flanagan, I just want to say that it's great to know that we can sleep sound in our beds at night with men of your calibre looking after our welfare and seein' to it that whiskey on which the duty hasn't been paid doesn't flood the land and do the Government out of their pound of flesh."

"Quite right Paddy. Where would we be without law and order and isn't it nice to know how much we're appreciated," he waved his empty glass at Bella, followed immediately by Maguire and Staunton. She glanced at her father who rolled his eyes, nodded and muttered, "Talk about payin' for protection."

"What was that Gleeson?"

"Ah, I was just wonderin' if yiz were stayin' for the election?"

"What election?"

"We're electin' a new King of Inishard on Friday. It's over three months now since Liam passed on, God rest his soul."

They all blessed themselves.

"Naw we can't come to that Paddy, we're raidin' Colls of Magheroarty on Friday and... aw shite... not a word now, do ye hear me, not a word," he wagged his finger at Paddy and glanced around furtively to see if anyone else had picked up on his faux pas. No one heard, but they would shortly.

The door opened and a dapper little sparrow of a man swaggered in. He wore a 'Robin Hood' hat, a long and loud check jacket in shades of blue, tight jeans and pointy-toed shiny shoes. A pencil moustache decorated his upper lip. On seeing the Guards, he paused, swept off his hat and gave an exaggerated bow and jauntied up to the bar.

"Holy God," the Sergeant muttered.

"Aye, Holy God," his subordinates echoed.

"Who the hell is that Paddy?"

"That, Sergeant, is Freddie Jackson from London town. He's here to service the light."

"He looks like one of those spivs in the fillums."

Freddie leered at Bella who was drying glasses, "Allo Bella me dahlin' - tickle me awse wiv a fevva."

"What did you say Jackson?" she squealed, swinging around to glare at him.

He looked at her with big innocent eyes, "Oi sed, it's partickerly nawsty wevva."

The man beside him choked on his Guinness and had to have his back slapped.

"And now my angel, a pint of the black stuff for the love of your life."

Freddie was married with kids but that hindered him not a jot in his quest to bed as many girls or women as he could. He wasn't having much luck with Bella though. Ah well, he would keep trying.

A while later the pub door clicked open again and a man slid in, a man who looked nervous, a man who hated to be noticed, a man with something to hide. The Sergeant's hackles rose, he could smell a law-breaker a mile off. He hissed to his men, "Staunton, Maguire, take a look at yer man who just came in. Ah for the love of Jaysus would yiz sit down," he put his head in his hands in exasperation at the two lads who had leapt to their feet to get a better look. He beckoned them closer and whispered, "Yer man that just came in. Did yiz notice anythin' out of the ordinary about him?"

The two youthful heads wagged in unison.

"If youse were as sharp as me, yiz would have noticed a bottle in a brown paper bag shticking out of hee's coat pocket. I'll bet me stripes that it's poitín. Wait, houl' yer wheesht, he's comin' this way. Leave this to me."

As the suspect passed by carrying a half pint of Guinness, the Sergeant leapt to his feet and pulled the bag out of the man's pocket. Everyone in the bar turned around to watch. "Aha, what have we here, my lad? Why don't we have a little look," and from the brown bag he pulled out a whiskey bottle about a quarter full. He showed it to his two colleagues and smiled triumphantly, then addressed the assembly. "I would suspect that no duty has been paid on this little lot. Your name my lad?"

"O'Callaghan sir. Seamus O'Callaghan."

"Address?"

"Inishard sir."

"Right O'Callaghan, if this is what I think it is, you're in trouble." He handed the bottle to Staunton. "Taste that, Albert."

Bella had his first name.

"I'd not be a great expert at poitín," Staunton whispered.

"Oh Jaaz, give it to me," the Sergeant pulled it out of his hand and took a small swig, swilled it around in his mouth, made a face and spat it on the floor.

"Ah Jeez Christ, that's awful, worst I ever tasted, not that I tasted much mind, but that stuff would blister paint. Garda Maguire, take charge of the evidence, mark it with the date, the time, the place and the name of the man we seized it from, Seamus O'Callaghan, a native of Inishard."

He turned slowly and beamed at Paddy and his committee. "Well, well, well, success at last Gleeson. Fourteen long years comin' to this island and I have me first case. The Super's goin' to be delighted with me, and he'll be so delighted that he'll be writing a wee love letter to you O'Callaghan, to meet him for a nice cup of tea in the courthouse on a date to be decided."

His men chuckled and looked admiringly at their Sergeant.

"Why don't youse lads go behind the counter and go through them bottles t'see if Mr. Gleeson here has been tempted to offer any of that 'paint stripper' for sale."

The young Gardaí couldn't believe their luck, and hurrying behind the bar they entered the domain of the glorious Bella. They were finding it hard to concentrate on the job in hand, as her perfume, her earthiness and her voluptuous presence rendered the discovery of poitín unimportant when a seizure had already been made and man's second basic instinct took over. Maguire, the more worldly of the two, had his own girl-friend and so was slightly less susceptible to Bella's charms, but Staunton blushed every time she caught him looking at her. He would have been thrilled to know that it was his name she had written on a beer mat, now nestling in her purse, for possible future reference.

"And now Mr. Gleeson, one for the road," said the Sergeant, finding it hard to stop smiling. These damned islanders had been making a fool of him forever, but he had them now. He sipped his brandy as his men rattled bottles around the shelves, showing no particular interest in their job. When he had drained his glass, he levered himself out of his chair, and called his men. "Right lads, I take it yiz found nothing, so c'mon. Before we go, and I am now addressing all of ye in this bar. Ye can spread the word far and wide that nobody outwits Michael J. Flanagan. Let the lawbreaker quake in he's shoes when the name of Flanagan is mentioned. Now, as you may have heard, the Gardaí is sometimes accused of inactivity, and of being, believe it or not, a bit thick. Well, I'll let yiz into a secret. These vacant looks on our faces are carefully cultivated to lull the unsuspecting lawbreaker into a false sense of security, so he gets careless, and then we pounce. Ye saw the results of it yourselves here today, in the swift and cunning seizure of illicit liquor from Mr. Seamus O'Callaghan."

He nodded beaming around the room and put on his cap.

"Well, goodbye Gleeson, thanks for the drinks, and here's something ye might keep in mind. Ye think ye're cute hoors up here in Donegal, but ye've a long way to go, to be as cute a hoor as a Kerry man," and he exited, laughing, his men hurrying after him with backward wistful glances at Bella.

As soon as the door closed, everybody looked at O'Callaghan who was sitting quietly by the window, watching the Gardaí marching down the pier towards their boat.

Paddy rounded on him. "In the name of Jaysus Seamus, what sort of an arse are ye, bringing that stuff in here. And you even saw them sittin' there, and you still wandered in like a pregnant duck with a bottle stickin' out of your pocket, have you lost your friggin' mind?"

O'Callaghan looked at him calmly. "It's ok Paddy. Wind your neck back in. They have no case."

"Whadya' mean they have no case. Haven't they got your bottle?"

"They have, but it's not poitín"

"What the hell is it then?"

"Well, y'see, I have a wee problem with the oul' water-works and the nurse asked me to bring her up a sample, so I got this oul' empty whiskey bottle and," he mimed urinating in the bottle.

The bar erupted.

CHAPTER EIGHT

DAN MEETS OWEN

The fishermen crowded into the pub for a well-earned pint or two after a long day out at sea. There was loud chatter and banter and Bella was flat-out, being the only one working. Paddy was in the mainland collecting supplies and Peter doing his usual job of bringing the empty glasses back behind the bar and washing them. After the first couple of thirst-quenching pints, and shared news of the days happenings, things calmed down a bit and the noise became more subdued.

One of the fishermen, a strong looking man, about thirty years old was sitting at a table by himself. He drained his glass, slammed it on the table and called, "Who'll buy a drink for the best buckin' man on Inishard?"

After some hesitation one of the men shouted, "Bella, set one up for Owen O'Gallachoir, the next King of Inishard."

There was a muted cheer at that pronouncement and they

turned back to the bar counter to carry on their conversation and enjoy their pints. Bella poured the pint and brought it over to Owen's table and set it down, whereupon he grabbed her by the waist and pulled her down on his knee, and tried to kiss her, at the same time roughly groping her breasts.

"Cut it out Owen, cut it out!" She twisted out of his grasp and stood up, breathing hard and very angry. "Don't be such a pig Owen. What makes you think you can get away with treating me like that. I'll not have anyone slobbering over me half-drunk and in your case make that sober as well."

There was silence as the patrons watched the drama unfold. Owen laughed derisively. "Yer free enough with other men. What's wrong with me? And I'm hearing you're making sheep's-eyes at that buck from America or wherever he's from."

"Mind your own bloody business Owen and keep your hands to yourself. And I'm not afraid of you either, like your so-called friends."

Owen was getting excited at the physicality of the exchange and stared at Bella's heaving bosom which was at his eye-level and temptingly close. "Oh, c'mon now darlin', there's no need to be so unfriendly. I'm not all that bad, and I happen to know that when a woman says 'no' she means 'yes'," and he grabbed her again, pulled her back down on his knee, held her face between his hands and forcibly kissed her, then shoved her to the ground where she landed on her hands and knees.

There was absolute silence as she got slowly to her feet, dusted down her apron, then spun around and hit him hard across the face with her fist. He jumped to his feet looking murderous, then realising where he was, he paused, and looked around to see every eye on him. Bella was standing right in front of him with an empty pint glass gripped in her hand, daring him to retaliate. After a moment, he decided to make light of the situation and gave a mirthless laugh.

"Ah Bella, God help the man that gets you, for he won't have his troubles to seek. Sure, I was only jokin'. Now away there and get the lads a drink. The drinks are on Owen O'Gallachoir," he shouted, and sauntering up to the bar he put his arms around the shoulders of two of his fellow fishermen, smiling and trying to be likeable but fooling nobody.

His three lukewarm supporters worked on the same fishing boat as him and it was easier to humour the skipper by agreeing with everything that he said than risk the fallout from his explosive temper. Bella had composed herself again and started serving the men when Owen demanded silence and addressed the company. "Don't forget now lads how to vote on Friday night. There's only Sean Mary Doohan stannin' agin me, and he's as oul' as tae in a mug. It'll be no contest at all. I can read and write as good as he can. Of course, yiz all know it's only a matter of time 'til I waltz the school teacher up the aisle, and Miss Siobhan Gray will become Mrs. Owen O'Gallachoir."

He looked around for a reaction, which after an embarrassing short silence was broken by his cronies who applauded enthusiastically which prompted the others join in half-heartedly.

Bella stared at him, fascinated.

"The two of us'll have no bother fillin' in them complicated forms the Council sends out every time we want somethin', and yiz'll be proud when yiz see our picture in the 'Journal' smilin' out at ye, with the writin' above it, sayin' 'The King of Inishard and his bride'. Now, would yiz be proud if ye had to look at a photie of Sean and Cathleen Doohan's ugly oul' mugs starin' back at ye?"

There was genuine amusement at that idea, and Owen, encouraged, warmed to his theme. "Now, as King I'd want a few improvements made to my house and I'd want the electric put in, for entertain' important visitors an' stuff like that."

Then he said what he thought would impress them, "I'll make sure we get every benefit I can squeeze outta the Council," he banged the table, "the Gaeltacht," he banged the table again, "and the Government." He banged the table one last time and waited for a reaction.

There was polite applause from everyone, as this aspiration was 'a consummation devoutly to be wished', but the doubt that Owen could fulfill these election promises was evident.

"I was thinkin' that when I'm elected, I'd give up the fishin' and we'll get a new teacher for the school, and me and Siobhan will spend our time travellin' to Belfast or Dublin or wherever, on your behalfs. I'll be pesterin' the County Council for grants for a big ferry to bring hundreds of tourists to the island, and I'll be talkin' to big businessmen, for we'll need a hotel to put the visitors in, all sorts of things like that. Them's just me startin' plans. What would Sean Mary do for the island? Nothin'. He's too old and set in he's ways. There's only one man on this island who deserves to be the King and who can deliver, and you're lookin' at him."

His crewmen clapped furiously and once again were rewarded with polite applause from the others. They were trying to imagine life on board a half-decker fishing boat with Owen if he failed to be elected King. He would probably blame them. He would certainly blame somebody. Even on the boat when things went wrong it was never his fault. A frayed rope that snapped, pots laid in the wrong place, an engine that died as the fuel filter hadn't been checked. Whatever it was, it was never Owen's fault.

Owen was disappointed by the reaction to his speech which he had spent a lot of time thinking out. He had had visions of being carried shoulder-high out of the pub and through the village with people cheering, waving, smiling and chanting 'Owen for King' but he suddenly became afraid that he hadn't stirred them up enough and those useless feckers he was counting on hadn't pulled their weight. He had done his best, buying drinks, laughing louder than anyone else and smiling more than anyone had ever seen him do before, but it didn't seem to be working. His conviction that he would be the next King was suffering a set-back and the doubt didn't do his temper any good.

Peter came from behind the bar with a bucket to collect the empty bottles and glasses, and a cloth to wipe the tables. He avoided eye-contact with Owen who glared at him.

"An' who are you gonna' vote for little man?"

Peter continued wiping the tables and becoming frightened, knowing that when Owen started with his insults, something bad was going to happen.

Owen thought he would amuse the patrons again and shouted, "Do we allow half-wits to vote in this election?"

There were strained guffaws from the cronies, but silence from the others as they turned slowly to regard Peter and Owen. They wouldn't interfere unless it became very serious. Peter quickly went back behind the bar where Bella would look after him.

Owen wouldn't let it go. "Look at him. In there trying to rub against Bella. Dirty wee brute."

Bella was coming back to boiling point, "Shut your foul mouth and leave Peter alone or I'll have ye put out and barred."

"Oh aye, you and what army? Maybe you like him in there rubbin' agin' ye. Maybe you're funny that way. No time for a man like me," he sniggered at his pals, "but she likes half-wits."

Owen got up and headed for the bar counter.

Peter dashed for the door and Owen stuck out his foot and tripped him.

"Watch where you're going you stupid wee runt."

Peter fell heavily just as the door opened and Dan stood there.

Bella yelled, "You're a real bastard Owen."

Dan helped Peter to his feet, who ran out the door past him. Dan glared angrily at Owen, "What the hell's going on here?"

Owen walked over to Dan and shoved his face inches from Dan's. "Who wants to know smart-arse? Wait, I know who you are, you're that buck from America or Australia or somewhere like that, right? Livingstone?"

"It doesn't matter who I am. What does matter is that you're bullying a gentle little guy like Peter. You should be ashamed of yourself whoever you are. Next time pick on someone your own size."

"Oh yeah? Like you, f'rinstance?"

Dan nodded, his temper just under control, "Yeah! Exactly like me."

They continued to stare at one another, neither of them knowing quite what to do next. Bella leaned over the bar and intoned in a faux-polite voice, "Mr. Dan Livingstone, meet Mr. Owen O'Gallachoir."

Dan's calm, unwavering gaze made Owen break eye contact first and he turned away and went back to his table with a "Humph." But he was aware of the presence and physicality of Livingstone, a man who would not be messed with. He could see that under Livingstone's polite exterior there was a man who probably knew how to use his fists.

Dan walked over to the bar, the men moving back to allow him in, "Bella, I'll have a glass of Guinness please."

Bella poured his drink and he took it and went to his usual table overlooking the harbour.

Owen had lost face again and he was angry. He stared at Dan, wanting to bring him down a peg or two and unable to let the matter drop, he followed him over to the table and towered over him. "Mr. Livingstone, the flower-man. Oh, yoohoo! Are ye one o' them nancy boys we've heard about?"

The patrons moved back expecting a fight. Two big men, one insults the other, a definite fight. But Dan just smiled and ignored Owen. Owen tried again. "Haven't you the right cheek on ye. A couple of days on the island and you're telling us how to behave, eh? Well, I'm telling you now, keep your fuckin' nose out of our business or else."

Dan got slowly to his feet, and the crowd moved back again. A fight was on for sure and they protected their drinks. "Or else what?"

"Never mind what. Just stay outta' my way and don't interfere in my business. And another thing, ye were seen makin' up to Siobhan Gray. Well, she's spoken for and she's marryin' me. And I hear you were playin' up to Bella before that. The cheek o' ye. If ye bucks think ye can come to our island and get off with our women, yiz have another think comin'. Don't ever let me hear of you cosyin' up to my fiancée, ever again, or you'll be sorry," with that he turned on his heel and nodding at his shipmates to follow him, he barged out of the door.

Most of the others drifted out shortly after, disgusted that they didn't get a fight, and their opinion of Dan slumped. Any man who could take insults like that and not retaliate must be a coward.

Bella came over to Dan's table and sat down. "Sorry about all that Dan. Owen's a bit jarred and when he's jarred, he's mean. When he's sober, he's not so bad. But when he gets an idea into his head, there's no changin' him. That's the way he is."

"Is he really engaged to Siobhan Gray?"

"Not at all. He wants her alright, he told her so. Told her

he was goin' to marry her and they'd make a great team. He still can't figure out why she wasn't delighted at the idea. He can't think of one reason why she'd refuse an offer from, in his opinion, the most eligible man on the island. Not at all, she'll never marry him. That fact hasn't thunk into his sick head yet, and when it does. What did I just say? I meant 'sunk into his thick head'!"

He grinned and she made a face, "They're both right, I think. Anyway, when he realises the truth," she puffed her cheeks and shook her head despairingly.

Dan couldn't see how this man would appeal to Siobhan in any way at all and wondered at his certainty that she was going to be his bride. He decided it was time to ask about his brother. "Bella, did you meet Richard Hilliard when he was here?"

She looked at him sharply, "How do you know Richard?"

"Well, we grew up together as kids. His parents knew I was coming here and asked me to make a few enquiries as they haven't heard from him in a while. Maybe he told somebody here what his plans were, where he was going next, that sorta' thing?"

Bella shook her head, "No I never heard him mention that. He didn't seem to be in any hurry to leave. He was great craic and full of stories about strange places in the world, and, why don't you talk to Siobhan about him. They spent a good bit of time together. I left the island on the mailboat to visit relations on the mainland for a few days and when I got back, I found out that he had gone, not left the island I mean, just disappeared. They searched for him but found nothing."

"Had people any idea why he might have disappeared?"

Bella shrugged, "Nobody seems to know. One day he was here, the next day he was gone. There were wild rumours of course."

"Like what?"

"Oh, that he fell off the cliffs, he drowned out swimming, some said he might have been a spy and was picked up by a submarine. Wild stuff like that. I heard that two men came over to see him from the mainland the day before he disappeared."

"Two men came to see him! I wonder what that was about. Do you know Bella?"

"I haven't a clue Dan. No idea. Well as I said, talk to Siobhan, she was here and they all went to a ceili together the night before he disappeared. She'll definitely know more than me."

"Thanks Bella, I'll talk to her."

Bella went back to the bar, and while Dan pondered this information, a bearded man left the bar and walked over towards Dan's table and looked out the window, not looking at Dan at all, and spoke quietly, "Mr. Livingstone, I heard you asking Bella about Mr. Hilliard. We're not certain but if I was you I would..." The door opened noisily and Owen entered the bar again, stopped and looked at Dan and at the man standing close to him who turned away and made his way out the door, nodding at Owen as he passed.

Owen ordered a drink at the bar and sat with his back to Dan, who realised that whatever warning or information the man had was unlikely to be passed on now. Dan couldn't help thinking that Richard's disappearance had something to do with Owen. He would talk to Siobhan tomorrow. Dan finished his drink and left, smiling at Bella as he went.

CHAPTER NINE

THE PICNIC

Dan and Siobhan trudged up the slopes to the south cliffs carrying a picnic hamper and a rug. The weather continued to hold and there was only a light breeze. Siobhan looked around and announced,

"This'll do."

She spread the rug and she and Dan sat down. He opened the hamper and she set out the food and drinks on the rug. He watched her, admiring her gentle actions, her lovely face, and the white filmy dress she wore on this occasion. She in turn stole glances at his handsome face, his curly black hair, his blue penetrating eyes, his khaki shirt with breast-pockets, the khaki shorts which revealed strong tanned legs with their downy cover of sun-bleached hair, and admitted to herself that if he tried to kiss her, she would find it hard to resist reacting enthusiastically.

She looked around, "This is one of the nicest spots on the

island. Sheltered from the North and East, an ideal spot for our picnic."

"You chose it well, I see it's sheltered from the nosey neighbours in the village as well."

Siobhan laughed as she poured tea into two cups.

"Well, of course, unless you think I should have invited them as well. Anyway, I see enough of them. Milk and sugar?"

"Yes please, one sugar and a splash of milk. Ah, this is lovely. A lovely day, a lovely place, a lovely girl."

She smiled and thought 'a bit corny, but I like it'. He carried on, "One of the things that impresses me, is generally speaking, the very laid-back attitude of the people to everything it seems. I thought that we Aussies were laid-back, but you lot put us in the shade. Is there any word in the Irish language which equates to the Spanish 'mañana'?"

She paused and looked thoughtful, "No, I don't think so. Nothing that would indicate that degree of urgency."

Dan laughed out loud. "So, what are the islanders really like?"

Siobhan sipped her tea and nibbled a sandwich as she put her thoughts together, "They're very private really. Very suspicious, very loyal to each other. Self-preservation and mutual protection are instinctive here and asking questions here about things they consider to be their own business is a waste of time. The Mafia's code of 'Omerta' is alive and well and living in Inishard. They're also very primitive in ways. Our legends say that years ago, while travelling in to the island, a priest no less, fell overboard from a half-decker. The boat wasn't going to stop and save him, and only outrage from the passengers who weren't islanders, forced the skipper to turn around and pick him up."

"You're joking!"

"No, no, not at all. You see that they believe that as they get their living from the sea, then it has the right to demand an occasional sacrifice. I even heard that if someone fell overboard and managed to cling to a rock, that his cries for help would be ignored, for whoever saved him would be the sea's next victim. Worse than that, if that man managed to make the shore, it was whispered that he would be beaten and returned to the water. Isn't that horrible? I don't know if those stories are true, but if so, they happened in the bad old days, couldn't happen nowadays, right? But just in case, don't fall into the sea Dan."

"I'll try not to. Next question, why have some of the men got ladies names, like Sean Mary Doohan?"

"Aye, it must sound funny to strangers, but if two men have the same name, which often happens, then his mother or father's name is inserted to differentiate between the two."

Dan pursed his lips and nodded, "Ah, now I get it. To change the subject. I'm not certain that we should be here together at all. I am told in the village that you are already spoken for."

Siobhan looked up, "And who, pray, told you that?"

"None other than your fiancé himself, Mr. Owen Gallagher. It's pronounced O'Gallaquire or something like that."

She looked angry, "The name first then the facts. In English it's Gallagher, in Irish it's 'O'Gallachoir' pronounced 'O'Gallakore' with a huchh on the 'K'."

"A what, a huchh?"

"It would take too long to explain and unless you're planning to learn our native tongue. And by the way, my name is spelled S-I-O-B-H-A-N. There's no 'V' in Irish. It's the Irish version of 'Joan'."

"I didn't know that. Anyhow, Owen warned me to stay away from you or face the consequences. I got the impression that he was serious. How come he believes you and he are a couple?"

A shadow passed over Siobhan's face, and she put her hand on Dan's arm. "Dan, watch Owen. I think he's a bit unhinged. When I first came here and met him at a ceili I thought he was very nice, quite handsome, attentive and charming. We danced several times together, but I did notice that when other men asked me to dance, he didn't look happy, and I suppose I was a bit flattered at that. He walked me home and was a perfect gentleman, shaking hands as he left me at the door. At the second ceili I noticed that I wasn't being asked to dance by any of the men, and little warning bells began to ring. The other men didn't seem to want to catch my eye. It looked like they had been warned off. Owen was becoming too attentive, too possessive. When he walked me home that time, he tried to get fresh. I laughed him off, but he wasn't taking no for an answer and in fighting him off I'm afraid I lost my temper with him and called him a lot of names I hadn't used in public before. It was a night to forget."

A tear trickled down her cheek at the memory, and Dan took one of the napkins and gently mopped it away. "A nasty kettle of fish, isn't he? Tell me more about him."

"Peter and Owen are brothers, or maybe half-brothers"

"What!"

"Hard to believe, I know. Their mother is the priest's housekeeper, Madge. Her husband was a fisherman who was lost at sea and after he died, she went to work for the priest. Peter was born about eight months later. Madge says prematurely, but as you can expect, tongues began to wag. It looks like Owen preferred to believe the rumour-mongers, and that's why he hates Peter, and his mother. Owen was very close to his father and was bereft when he was drowned. He had been close to his mother too, but when Peter came along that all changed. I can understand his anger and feel a bit sorry for him. Being stuck on a small island in those circumstances with those rumours flying around has obviously affected him. I see Madge looking at him with a terrible sadness on her, and I suppose he bullies Peter to get back at her for her perceived infidelity and disloyalty to his father."

"And what do you think Siobhan?"

"I wish I knew Dan. All I can say is that Madge was horrified at the rumours and I'm told that Fr. O'Dwyer spoke out from the pulpit shortly after Peter was born and angrily berated those in his congregation who were spreading them, that Madge O'Gallachoir was one of the most honourable women he had ever met, and that those people should be ashamed of themselves for their wagging tongues which were destroying her reputation, her husband's memory, and causing discord in her family. But alas the rumours had had their effect."

She paused again and Dan sat quietly, sipped his tea and waited. She had more to say. "I suppose Peter could have been born prematurely, or maybe she did have a fling with a man after her husband died, maybe even the priest, both of which are very unlikely, but that suspicion still lasts to this day, with the priest theory at the top of the list I may add."

Dan frowned. "I can see why Owen is an angry man. But at the time did he or someone else go to the church higher-ups and have the matter investigated?"

"I would have thought so, and if it was investigated, and Fr. Tom is still here, then he was obviously exonerated and allowed to stay. You haven't met him yet Dan?"

"Not yet."

"Well, you will, and I'd be surprised if you don't like him. Everybody likes Fr. Tom. He's open and funny and involved in everybody's life. He doesn't walk around praying all the time, not one of those pious priests. He's more likely to be found any day sitting in somebody's kitchen, with his feet at the fire and a mug of tea or something stronger in his hand, talking about the things that concern that household."

"He sounds like a nice guy. I look forward to meeting him. To get back to Owen, you've made it clear Siobhan how you feel?"

"Of course I have. After the incident where I had to fight him off, he calmed himself and appeared to be sorry. He sought out my company and continued to tell me what a fine couple we'd make. At the start I tried to let him down gently, but that didn't work, so I made it very clear that he was wasting his time. I told him to look elsewhere for a wife and went into detail as to why were not in any way suited. I might as well have been talking to the wall, he just smiled and wasn't taking in what I was saying, my words didn't fizz on him."

"Fizz on him?"

She laughed, "Sorry, it just a local expression meaning that what I saying wasn't getting through. Anyhow, that's enough about him. What about you? Apart from a few basic facts I know nothing about you. For instance, I don't even know if you're married."

He quickly put his right hand over his left, by the way to hide a ring on his finger and tried to look guilty. She swung a playful slap at him. He pulled back out of reach and smiled. "No, I am not married, never have been. But that doesn't make me a confirmed old bachelor. I'm a bit fussy you see, I'm waiting on the right girl to come along. Maybe I'll meet her someday," and he smiled and stared off into the middle distance.

She frowned.

He continued, "Actually, I've been so busy working that I haven't had time to acquire a mate."

"Oh, so that's how it is, acquire a mate is it? Like 'acquiring' a car or a new suitcase. Is that how you see a wife? Just something that one should 'acquire' to make one's life complete, to serve one's meals and darn one's socks and maybe give one children to perpetuate one's ..."

Dan laughed and raised his hand "Hold on there, young lady! I can see plainly I'm going to have to choose my words very carefully when you're around. And with that in mind I have a question for you Miss Gray. Have you ever been, or intend to be, married?"

"You're very inquisitive Mr. Nosey Parker, but since you answered my question, I'll answer yours. No, I've never been married or even engaged, but I did think seriously about it once, when I was teaching in London. You're not a botanist at all, are you Dan?"

He drew back startled. "What makes you say that?"

"Because I asked you if you had found Oncidium growing on the cliffs, and you said 'not yet'. A botanist would have known that Oncidium, the Butterfly Orchid, can only be found at least a thousand miles south of here in the tropics."

"Blast. I didn't expect to find anybody here who would know plants. Have you a degree in botany as well?"

"Nothing like that, I'm just a keen gardener and only the day before I had read about Oncidium in a gardening magazine. I was just teasing you, expecting you to contradict me, and when you didn't, I knew you were either a very bad botanist, or too mannerly to point out my mistake, or thirdly, you weren't a botanist at all. I figured it was the third one. Who are you Dan and why are you here pretending to be something you're not?"

Dan swallowed the last of his tea, lit a cigarette and leaned towards her. "Just a couple of months ago, a man called Richard Hilliard came to Inishard and hasn't been seen since. I've come to find out what happened to him, if I can, or where he went after he left here. You and he were friendly I hear. My name is Dan Hilliard."

She stared at him. "Of course. You're his brother. I can see the resemblance now. He mentioned he had a brother who was a pilot."

Dan nodded and laughed, "I hope I'm a better pilot that I am a botanist. I thought I'd change my name in case people who might know something would clam up, and being a botanist would let me amble around without raising suspicion. So, tell me Siobhan what happened when Richard got here."

"I met Richard shortly after he arrived and found him very interesting. I can't get over that you're his brother. My God. Not that you're not very interesting as well. You are. Anyway, he was good fun, loved to laugh and was very outgoing. There was no particular chemistry or anything like that between us, it was just good to talk to someone who had a wide knowledge of so many things, and we enjoyed each other's company. Then a few days after he arrived, we were sitting chatting above the pier when two men arrived on the mail-boat from Bunbeg. They didn't look like islanders. They were better dressed and wore hats instead of caps. One was in his mid-fifties I would say, and the other a bit younger. As they walked up the pier towards us, they paused when they saw Richard. Then they approached us and the older man excused himself and asked Richard if he was Mr. Hilliard. Richard in his usual easy way said "The same". The older man asked him politely if they could have a private word. "Of course," said Richard and told me that he would see me at the ceili that night, and the three walked off together. It was the day before Richard disappeared."

"Two men came looking for him! Did you see them again, or hear what they wanted to talk to Richard about?"

"Well partly. When I arrived at the ceili that night, they were there, sitting with Richard and they all seemed to be on friendly terms. He introduced them to me as Peadar and Liam, and whispered that he would tell me all about it later. The dancing started and we all had a great time doing 'Shoe the Donkey', the 'Siege of Ennis' and 'The Waves of Tory'.

Anyway, at that stage Owen arrived. He had been drinking. You could feel the atmosphere changing as he walked into the hall, but maybe that was just me. He made a bee-line for me when a dance was announced, but I made sure to grab Richard and drag him onto the floor before Owen got to our table."

"Did Owen dance at all, with anyone else?"

"I didn't see him dancing at all, but any time I spotted him he was staring at us. I thought it would be a good idea for me to slip away in case trouble started, so when I saw Grace Johnston my house-mate getting her coat, I said my good-nights to Richard, Peadar and Liam and left with her. That would have been about three in the morning."

"Did Owen see you go?"

"I couldn't see him in the hall, so I don't think so."

"Weren't you afraid that he was waiting for you outside?"

"I was a bit, but with Grace for company, I didn't expect any trouble."

Dan, with a sinking heart, felt that he was getting close to finding out why his brother disappeared. Everything was pointing at Owen or possibly the two visitors Peadar and Liam, but they seemed less likely suspects given their apparent friendliness towards Richard. "And then what?"

"Well, later that Saturday morning, about eleven, Grace came into my room to tell me that Richard hadn't returned to Keenans after the ceili, and that a search was underway for him. I can tell you Dan, my heart stopped and I leapt out of bed, dressed and joined one of the search parties which was just heading off to cover the southside of the island. Peadar and Liam were in that party. They were staying in Gleesons, and they seemed just as concerned as the rest of us. It was hoped that Richard might have had too much to drink, and was 'sleeping it off' in a ditch somewhere. The whole island was scoured by about five o'clock that afternoon, but there was no sign of Richard, and no boats had arrived or left the island as the seas were still high from the last big wind, so Fr. Tom rang the Guards in Bunbeg and four of them and a couple of plain-clothes men arrived the next afternoon when the boats had started running again, and another complete search was carried out."

"Did you talk to them?"

"I think they interviewed everybody on the island and the visitors who hadn't gone home yet, including me."

"Did you tell them about Owen and Peadar and Liam?"

"I did. They seemed to know Peadar and Liam though they didn't say how. Anyway, the upshot of it was Richard had disappeared there was no evidence of foul play, so nothing was done. They suggested that we keep searching, for if he had fallen into the sea and drowned, that he might re-appear and we should let them know."

"Where was Owen when the island was being searched?"

"With one of the search parties on the north end. I asked someone in that party, in a roundabout way or course, how he seemed, and it appears that he was just as concerned as everybody else. I saw him again when the Guards were there and we all searched the island and the shore again. He gave me an 'isn't it awful' look and said that he hoped 'poor Richard would turn up somewhere alive and well'."

There was a long silence as Dan took in all the information and tried to visualise what had actually occurred. Siobhan started slowly packing away the remains of the picnic, and then he asked her the question she was dreading. "What do you think happened Siobhan?"

She dropped her head and look agitated, then after a long pause, he reached out and took her hands in his, and her eyes filled with tears, "Oh Dan," she wept on his shoulder. His arm encircled her waist. "I've tried not to think about it. I don't want to think about it, and, it may have been an accident. He went for a walk on the cliffs and was blown over by the wind, simple as that. But every time I see Owen, oh God! Or maybe the two men who came to see him, but I don't think so."

Siobhan was reluctant to point an accusing finger, yet her suspicions spoke volumes. Dan was almost sure now that his brother was dead, and that he had died on this island, possibly murdered with one likely and two possible suspects. His own eyes filled up as the realisation hit him that he would never see the smiling face of his brother again.

They sat like that for a long time, her head on his shoulder, his arm around her waist, each lost in their own thoughts, his grief mingling with the completeness he felt for the girl in his arms, then he tipped her head back and kissed her gently on the lips. "Siobhan, I need to be alone for a while, would you mind? You go back to the village, I'll bring the hamper back."

"Of course, Dan."

"One thing I meant to tell you. A tall man with a beard approached me in the pub with some kind of warning, but he was interrupted when Owen came in, and he just walked away. Do you know who that might be?"

She thought for a moment and said, "That might be Sean. There are not many men around with beards, and he's not an islander, at least not from Inishard. He comes here now and again and chats to some of the locals, but nobody seems to know anything about him, just that his name is Sean. He might be an archaeologist or a writer or something, but he mostly keeps himself to himself. I've never spoken to him."

"Ok. I just wondered."

They stood up, she kissed him again and walked away.

CHAPTER TEN

THE ELECTION COMMITTEE

At eight o'clock on the Thursday evening Fr. Tom O'Dwyer was hosting a meeting in the Parochial House to go through the details of the following day's election with a committee of respected islanders and the two candidates, but Owen hadn't arrived yet. Sitting around the dining room table were John and Kathleen Keenan, Nurse Grace Johnston, Jack Shaughnessy, Paddy Gleeson and Sean Mary Doohan. Madge had prepared tea and sandwiches, and while they were eating, they talked about the gale forecast for the following evening and Saturday morning, and hoped that the boats from the other islands would get in with no bother tomorrow, Friday. The visiting boats might have to stay a day or two depending on the duration of the gale, but there was nothing unusual in that.

At half-past eight when they had finished their supper, there was still no sign of Owen. Madge was terrified of Owen coming to the priest's house for the first time since she had lost her husband, and of what he might say or do. She could see nothing but trouble ahead. She wasn't alone. Everyone there was on tenterhooks at the prospect.

Eventually Fr. Tom got to his feet. "Thank you all for coming. Owen hasn't sent in an apology for non-attendance, so we must presume he still intends to show up, but we can't wait any longer, so I call the meeting to order. Now, this last meeting is just to go over the plans again and make sure we've forgotten nothing, so a quick run through the agenda. First of all, catering, Nurse Johnston?"

"All organised Father. A bowl of vegetable soup when the guests arrive and after the election we'll serve tea, sandwiches, cake and pastries."

"Good, good, well done, and now John, the election details."

There was a collective silent groan. John Keenan was a lovely man, sincere but very painstaking and deliberate who it was believed, even by his wife, could 'bore for Ireland' if it ever became an Olympic event. 'Keeping it short' wasn't one of his gifts. He rose to his feet and coughed to clear his throat, "I'll be brief."

They looked at him in disbelief and hope.

"As everyone entitled to vote arrives, they will be given a voting slip with the names of the two candidates printed clearly thereon. Having visited several printing establishments and checked their prices, I eventually settled on Barr's Printers in Letterkenny who came in with the best price for one hundred and fifty voting slips, two pounds. Now when called upon to vote, the eligible person will enter a voting booth - we have three, as you know - he or she will mark their candidate of choice with an X, and then folding their slip, they will place it in the ballot box. This function will be personally supervised by myself. When all have voted, the ballot box will be emptied in a private place in the hall, where the persons here present will count and verify the result of the ballot, with the exception of Sean Mary here, who is of course a candidate, and would be debarred from taking part in the count, as would Owen of course being another candidate."

To everyone's relief Fr. Tom interjected, "Good man John, good man, thank you. We've a good idea how it's done. Is that all?"

John, a bit miffed at being cut off in mid-flow carried on. "When the votes have been counted, the result will be announced by yourself Father, and the new King presented with the royal sash, the traditional emblem which has been handed down..."

The priest interrupted again, "Good, excellent, thank you John. Now, Paddy, the entertainment?"

Paddy laughed. "We have so many people coming from the mainland and the islands bringing their pipes, tin whistles, fiddles, flutes and accordions, that it's an orchestra we'll have. Should be a great sound altogether. And we have powerful singers comin' too, and dancers as well. There's a lad coming from Gortahork with a guitar and a microphone." Paddy paused to let the enormity of that news sink in.

They all looked at one another with little nods of approval.

"A microphone how are ya. Now there's a first for Inishard and only possible since we got the generator. At two in the morning after the election should be over, the Chairman of Donegal County Council Mr. Paddy Friel, will ring your number Father to have a word with and congratulate the new King, so he'll have to be here to take that call. Now, regarding the refreshments, there will be plenty of tea and minerals for them as doesn't take a sup, and for them as does, that liquid refreshment will be provided by myself."

There was a commotion and raised voices coming from the kitchen, and they heard Owen shouting, "I'll come in if I like. They're expectin' me. I'm a fuckin' candidate amn't I?"

They heard Madge trying to calm him down. "Please Owen, you've been drinking, and remember it's the priest's house you're in."

"Get out of my friggin' way," a scuffle was heard and the door to the dining room was yanked open and Owen stood there, breathing hard and bleary-eyed, his mother behind him trying to pull him back into the kitchen.

Fr. Tom stood up and raised a hand to tell Madge that it was ok, he would deal with it. It was painfully obvious to everyone that Owen was very drunk

"I'm here for the meetin'."

"Owen, we waited as long as we could, the meeting is almost over now,"

Owen nodded, "Shawlmost over ish it? Yiz shouldn't a started it an' me not here, so yiz can bloody schtart again," he nodded to himself and sat heavily in a chair.

Fr. Tom addressed the others around the table. "Thank you all for coming. I think we have covered everything of importance," he tilted his head to indicate that they should go.

Paddy looked pointedly at him with a look that plainly said 'are you sure you don't want me to stay'?

Again, the priest gave him a little look of 'it's ok, you can go'. As they pushed back their chairs and prepared to go Owen became aware and sat up straight in his chair, "Hey. Hey! Where the fuck are yiz goin', I'm here fer the meetin', sit down, how dare yiz leave."

As the door closed behind them, Owen looked drunkenly around, "How dare yiz leave, amn't I a candidate and the besht buckin' man on Inishard. I'm a candidate. I'll show yiz, how dare yiz leave, whatsh wrong with me? Come back, come back!"

In the resulting silence he put his head in his arms and to the priest and his mother's surprise and dismay he started to sob. In the open door of the kitchen Madge stood looking at her son, heartbroken.

Fr. Tom moved by compassion put his hand on Owen's shoulder, "C'mon now Owen. You've a big day ahead of you tomorrow."

Owen staggered to his feet, knocking over his chair, and holding on to the table for support,

"Don't touch me. Leave me alone. Ye're always bloody preachin'. If you'd practish what you preach sometimes, we might lishen to you. 'No close dancin', it's a sin'," he says. Hah! What a joke. No close dancin' indeed," he leaned forward and glared into Fr. Tom's face. "If the Bishop knew half of what's goin' on here, you'd be shifted sideways Father O'Dwyer. And talking about fathers, why don't you come clean and tell us what we all know, that you're..."

Madge yelled, "Owen, how dare you talk to Fr. O'Dwyer like that, you brat. You think you've all the answers don't you! Did you ever think you might be wrong? Now, as your mother, I'm telling you to get out of this house, you and your foul mouth. Get out, now, now Owen."

Owen turned unsteadily and glared at his mother. "And fuck you too," he stumbled past her, shoving her hard against the wall and she fell to the floor as he made his way out into the kitchen, and they heard the back door banging closed.

Fr. Tom helped Madge to her feet and on to a chair. "Are you hurt Madge?"

"Me heart more than me head Father. God help him, he's very twisted. He was only nine when he lost his father, and then with Peter and the rumours, he's lost. Since he took to the drink and listening to the wrong people, he's getting worse and worse."

Father Tom sat down beside her and took one of her hands in his.

"Y'see Father, he's afraid of losing anything else he's set his heart on, like being King of Inishard, and marrying Siobhan Gray, and God help him he hasn't a hope of either. Peter tells me that Siobhan and Mr. Livingstone go walking every day, and Father, I'm afraid." Her tears started to flow again, "the same thing that happened Mr. Hilliard, could happen again."

Fr. Tom interrupted her, "Now, now, Madge. I've told you before, there's not a shred of evidence that anything happened to Mr. Hilliard at all at all. For all we know, he could be sitting in the south of France at this very moment drinking a good wine."

"Do you really think so Father?"

"Certainly, certainly. Now off with you woman, and make us both a nice cup of tea."

"I will. Thank you, Father. Thank you." She was grateful for Fr. Tom's comforting words, but in her heart, she didn't really believe them.

CHAPTER ELEVEN

ELECTION DAY

Next morning, Friday, election day, dawned bright and clear, but as the day progressed the clouds thickened and darkened and the air was still, the calm before the forecast storm. Islanders left their home ports in time to get to Inishard well before the weather broke. Jack Shaughnessy in the lighthouse kept a watchful eye as a small flotilla of half-deckers headed for his island, all of which arrived safely and were tied up inside the pier before 7p.m.

The Community Hall was full of people during the day, including Siobhan and Dan, putting up streamers, coloured electric bulbs, organising the tables and chairs, the voting booths, the catering corner, the big soup boiler, the gas rings, the teapots, the drinks counter and all the other bits and pieces which would be needed on this occasion.

The young man from Gortahork arrived with his guitar, microphone and two speakers, and he offered Fr. Tom the use of the mic, who was pleased that he would be heard without having to raise his voice for a change.

About ten o'clock the first heavy drops of rain were felt, followed by a rumble of distant thunder as people were getting ready to leave for the hall. The thunder got closer and louder and flashes of lightning streaked across the sky and the rain lashed down, turning the dirt road into a muddy walkway. Ladies who owned an umbrella realised that the wind was stronger that they thought it would be, as their umbrellas were quickly whipped inside out as they stepped out of their doorways. Coats and hats were gripped tightly as the wind whistled around the houses. The storm coming from the south crashed the waves against the pier and the spray ventured some distance inland. The newer houses on Inishard had slate roofs, but most had their original thatch which was well tied down against stormy weather.

Inside the hall, the gas heaters were on despite it being an August night, the curtains were closed and the large entrance porch where the wet coats were hung, kept the wind from flying directly into the main hall. It was colourful and cosy and the sturdy walls kept out most of the noise of the gale. The musicians had all congregated at the stage-end of the hall and the chairs were set around the walls three deep, with the centre kept open for dancing. Lively dance tunes greeted the smiling faces as they arrived and met their fellow islanders.

Men who only met up a couple of times a year crowded Paddy's bar, with each man insisting on buying the other a drink. Some of the visiting men had their wives with them as well, and huddles of married women caught up on the latest news and scandals while the unmarried girls were checking out the young men. The lad from Falcarragh with the guitar and microphone was getting many admiring glances, but he wasn't in the market and kept the lassies at a distance with his manner and obvious disinterest. His friend who helped him with his gear wouldn't have been amused otherwise.

At a regular dance in 1950's Ireland, the boys and girls didn't sit together. The girls lined one side of the hall and the lads lined the other and when the band struck up a modern tune, the bolder men charged across the floor to ask the girls of their choice to dance. They were usually successful and were much envied by the shyer boys who often spent a whole evening plucking up courage to 'cross the divide' even once. A 'Ladies Choice' took the pressure off, and many were surprised and pleased to be chosen to dance. The bands in those days were nearly always local and usually comprised a thin ancient drummer who looked like he had just backed a loser at the National, and who kept a monotonous beat and wouldn't dare attempt a flourish, a saxophone player with a pasty face and a comb-over, a stout lady with bat's wings flapping as she vamped on a jangly piano which was almost in tune, and a chubby ever-smiling piano-key accordionist who considered himself the band's front-man and sex symbol even though his teeth kept slipping.

Of course, at a ceili this dance-hall problem didn't apply. Everyone got on the floor and danced sets with multiple partners.

In the hall the voting was still going on and there was a great buzz of rapid Irish echoing around the room as the people of Inishard finished casting their votes and found a seat, everyone carrying their bowls of soup which were very welcome on such a night. When the two candidates Sean Mary Doohan and Owen O'Gallachoir arrived, they were given generous applause. The drinks table was busy with Paddy, Bella, Peter and two young islanders roped in to help, but when they reckoned that everyone was in, Paddy as 'Fear an Ti', the Man of the House, and the M.C. had to desert his bar and mount the stage. The two candidates were sitting on the stage on either side of Paddy who stood behind the centrally placed microphone.

"Quite please!" he shouted, nearly deafening everybody. The chatter stopped and everyone stared at him. Siobhan leaned into Dan to translate the speeches.

"Aw jaaz sorry, that made me jump too. I wouldn't be used to these things, can yiz hear me now at the back?"

Shouts of 'we can' answered him.

"Right so. Ladies and gentlemen, it's my pleasure as your host for the evening to welcome you all here on this great occasion and celebration on account of the fact that tonight Inishard will have a new King."

Cheers and applause greeted this pronouncement.

"We have two candidates for the post. On my right we have Owen O'Gallachoir, a young man with great plans for the Island, and who because of his youth, could be the King of Inishard for the next forty or fifty years."

The erratic applause reflected the realisation that Owen could be their spokesman for a long time to come.

"And on this side, we have Sean Mary Doohan who was a close friend of Liam McClafferty our last King, and who also has the welfare of the island and its people close to his heart."

The cheers and applause were much more enthusiastic.

"So, I suppose your choice tonight is, do ye want a new broom to sweep clean, or an old broom that's still serviceable."

Hoots of laughter greeted his description of the candidates.

"As I speak, the votes are being counted, and may the best man win."

The crowd applauded again.

"Among our distinguished guests here this evening is Mr. Dan Livingstone from Australia. We have Mr. and Mrs. Sean Ban Boyle and Mr. and Mrs. Eamon McClafferty, as well as

Peadar O'Donnell and two of his friends, Liam and Sean, all from Arranmore."

Dan looked over at the people from Arranmore Island and saw that the bearded man was one of them, Sean.

"As youse know, Eamon is a nephew of our late King, Liam McClafferty."

A respectful round of applause was given from the sympathetic gathering.

"We welcome all our friends from Bunbeg, Magheroarty, Burtonport, Falcarragh, Gweedore, in fact from all over the world and many other places besides. Now our principal guest tonight is the King of Tory Island, Padraig Óg Rodgers and his wife Breda."

The King of Tory stood up to great applause, and removed his cap and waved it, which indicated how important he felt this evening was. Very few people ever saw Padraig Óg with his cap off, and they got a rare glimpse at a very white bald dome topping a leathery weather-beaten face. It was rumoured that he kept the cap on in bed.

Paddy continued, "We did invite Sergeant Flanagan to come tonight, but for some reason he was unable to make it and told us so in words that Fr. Tom wouldn't know."

Roars of laughter greeted this remark, as they all knew the now-famous story of the 'seizure' of a few days earlier. "He's supposed to be leading a raid in Magheroarty tonight, but something tells me he won't be in charge of any raids tonight or any night, as he can't tell the difference between poitín and, well, you know. And here is the man who brought it all about, a man whose name will go down in the history of Inishard. Seamus O'Callaghan."

Seamus stood up beaming and waving as he was given a great cheer and even Fr. Tom was seen trying to smother a laugh.

"Now, I hope yiz voted early and voted often"

He was rewarded with a sprinkle of laughter at that old chestnut.

"When the votes have been counted and double-checked, we'll let ye have the result of the ballot. Now, the weather has let us down a bit, but I supposed we're used to that. Are we gonna' allow the weather to dampen our spirits?"

Roars of no answered him.

"Of course not. Now that ye've had your soup let's get the action started and I want to see everybody on the floor for 'The Waves of Tory'."

"Hup we get," laughed Siobhan to Dan "and let's see if you have a step in you."

"Wait a bit," protested Dan. "You go and I'll watch till I see how it's done."

"Righto," off she went making up a 'four' in preparation for the dance. The music started and away went the dancers with Dan studying the backwards and forwards movement of the lines, the breaking into 'fours' and 'twos', the side-stepping, the lines of dancers ducking and rising, making waves with their arms as they progressed up and down the floor, and the couples and fours swinging around at a great speed. The enthusiastic men in the 'fours' swinging around in a circle with their arms around each other's waists, often went so fast that the ladies feet left the floor and stuck out behind them. The dancers had hardly time to catch their breaths before the music started again and there followed waltzes, polkas and quicksteps.

Siobhan and Dan danced mostly together, but also with other partners. The local children performed a traditional jig and a couple of step dances, their little unsmiling faces concentrating like mad, their arms stiffly to their sides and their feet and legs twinkling around the floor. Then followed the 'Siege of Ennis' 'The Walls of Limerick' and another 'Waves of Tory' where Dan surprised Siobhan by being very good despite it being his first attempt. He was light on his feet and had a great sense of rhythm and timing. She loved to dance and was pleased that he seemed to enjoy it too.

Now and again, she would glance at Owen and her smile of pleasure quickly died when she saw the expression on his face, a combination of hate, fear and loss. She looked at Dan who seemed to be unconcerned, and was afraid for him. She wanted to get away from here, but knew she couldn't, just yet.

While the dancing was going on, the candidates stayed on the stage shaking hands with people, Sean Mary warmly and Owen with a strained distracted look, smiling with his mouth and making small-talk as he watched over crowding shoulders as his fiancée and that Australian bastard swung around the floor smiling and laughing, despite his warnings to them.

He still had hopes of being elected and after that he would put a stop to that behaviour. But then again, the stupid cow was allowing herself to be duped by that slick-talking stranger. Didn't she know that? He would dump her after he'd shagged her a few times and head off back to Australia, leaving her behind, maybe pregnant. He felt his anger growing at the idea, and of course he wouldn't marry her then, her disgrace would be known all over the place. Or maybe she would actually go to Australia with him. He suddenly realised that his plans for Siobhan and him were disintegrating before his eyes. He spotted his mother looking at him and when they locked eyes, she gave him a sad smile and he immediately looked away.

People bought drinks for the candidates, usually halves of whiskey which Owen quickly downed, while Sean Mary sipped and set most of the glasses to the side or passed them on to friends. At the end of a dance Paddy stepped back onto the stage and stood in front of the microphone.

"Quiet, quiet please."

The hubbub died down and everyone looked towards the

stage which had been vacated except for the two candidates, Fr. Tom and himself. "I have just been informed that the count has been completed and double-checked and the result of the ballot will be announced shortly after we have heard from a man who has been so long on Inishard that he's almost a native. Ladies and gentlemen, Fr. Tom O'Dwyer."

A huge round of applause greeted the priest as he stepped in front of the mic.

"Thank you, Paddy. Thank you, friends." He paused until he had complete silence. "Next month I will celebrate my silver jubilee as a priest and twenty three of those twenty-five years will have been spent with you here on Inishard."

A round of applause and a few whoops of support greeted his remark.

"As you may know, in our Church a priest who steps out of line is often sent by his Bishop to an out-of-the-way place, usually for a year or two to reflect on the folly of disagreeing with established practices. I will admit that there were matters where the Bishop and I didn't see eye to eye, so I was sent to Inishard to teach me a lesson."

Just then there was a boom of thunder close overhead and he looked heavenwards, smiled, pointed up and looked around the hall.

"Twenty-three years later it appears I still haven't learned my lesson."

Laughter and applause came from smiling, tough islanders.

"Anyway, enough of that. I just want you to know that I wouldn't want to be anywhere else."

The cheers and applause this time went on for at least a minute, and a smiling Fr. Tom had to raise his hands to get them to quieten down again. "Now then, back to the business of the evening, the election of a new King of Inishard. Our late lamented King, Liam McClafferty was King when I came to the island first. He was a thoughtful quiet man who worked hard for the welfare of not only this Island, but for all the islands around our coast and tonight I want you to show your appreciation for Liam to his wife Mary and his children Ruadhri, Seamus, Eilis and Eibhlin."

With one accord everyone got to their feet and facing the shy but smiling McClafferty family, clapped 'til their hands were sore.

Fr. Tom waited until the applause died down and went forward to the microphone again, taking a sheet of paper from his pocket. "And well deserved too. Thank you all. Now, the result of the election. There are one hundred and twelve people eligible to vote, and we had a one hundred percent turnout. The votes were cast as follows. Spoiled votes, six. One candidate polled twenty-two votes and the other polled eighty-four votes. Ladies and gentlemen please welcome your next King of Inishard," a pre-arranged fanfare was played on an accordion, "Sean Mary Doohan."

Sean Mary stood up, smiling and acknowledging the applauding crowd, then crossed over to Owen and shook hands with him. Fr. Tom continued, "Congratulations to both candidates who offered their time and talent for the benefit of you all, but as we know there can only be one winner and, on this occasion, experience was chosen over youth."

Owen felt sick, but with all eyes on him he forced a smile and returned Fr. Tom's handshake. Having foreseen the result, he acted like a good loser and congratulated Sean Mary and left the stage shaking sympathetic hands as he made his way slowly to the back of the hall. Calls of 'speech, speech' brought Paddy back to the stage.

"Yes, yes you'll have a speech but first we have to swear in our new King, Sean Mary. This duty will be performed by the Sacristan, Mr. John Keenan. John."

Everyone sat down as John stepped up to the mic. Sean

Mary stood centre stage as John Keenan opened a small very old leather case and took out a faded green linen cape with little gold tassels and placed it around the new King's shoulders, then cleared his throat. "Ladies and gentlemen, this cape has been worn and these words have been used for many generations in the swearing in of a new King. In this day and age, they may be a bit out of date, but as they're part of our tradition we'll continue to use them."

He unrolled a yellowed scroll and intoned, "May the ancient mysteries of the Lands of this World, and the seas below the land, and the Heavens above the land be revealed to you. May the Spirits of our ancestors guide you. May you live long among your people dispensing wisdom and justice without fear or favour. May Columcille and all the Saints in Heaven guide your steps and protect you from the wrath of Balor. Through Jesus Christ or Lord. Amen."

He shook hands with Sean Mary who walked to the microphone during the applause. "Thanks very much everyone. I am very happy to have inherited the title of the poorest King of the smallest nation in the world, but it's still a great honour. I'd like to echo the words said in praise of Liam who held this office for thirty years and did it wisely and well. Big shoes to fill. In the early days the main qualification to be King was to be able to read and write, to fill in forms or to read a letter from a loved one living in Canada, or America, or England, of Scotland or in any part of the wide world. Then when night fell, we would gather and sit at a fireside in a crowded house and Liam would read to us the works of Defoe, O'Casey, Dickens, MacPeadair, O'Connor, or maybe just the latest happenings in the local newspapers. In those early days we had no resident priest. They only came once a week, weather permitting, to say Mass and hear confessions Now we have our own Chapel and our own priest, a school, and a dispensary, a good pier and electric light, and we can all read and write in Irish. Most of us can speak in English, except for the wanes. We've come a long way in the last few years, and many of our men would be qualified in the reading and writing department to take on the responsibility of King," he pointed at men surrounding the stage, "men like Owen there, or Paddy, or John, or Seamus and others. Anyway, it's my duty now, and I will do what I can to live up to your confidence in me, and my door is always open."

There was generous applause from people who liked Sean Mary and were relieved that Owen didn't get in. Sean Mary turned to Fr. Tom, "I would ask Fr. Tom for his blessing."

Everyone, sitting or standing bowed their heads and crossed themselves as the priest spoke.

"In the name of the Father and the Son and the Holy Spirit, Amen. Dear Lord look kindly on this man and give him strength and wisdom to deal with the trials and tribulations of the days ahead. Guide his footsteps in Thy path and grant that he may do Thy will. We ask your blessing on him and on all here present, this night and forever more."

Everyone murmured 'Amen' and blessed themselves again.

Paddy moved to the mic. "Thank you, Father. Now I would like youse all to stand now and raise your cups glasses mugs or whatever you have, in a toast to Sean Mary Doohan, the King of Inishard."

An enthusiastic toast was drunk and applauded.

Paddy called out, "Music maestro, please," and the party continued. The nurse, Grace, grabbed Dan. and pulled him out on the floor for an old-time waltz.

"You can't hog him all night," she laughed to Siobhan, as they took to the floor. Siobhan shrugged, smiled at them and turned around to find Owen standing in front of her.

"Will you dance?"

Her first thought was to refuse him, but realised that it

would look bad, and he had already had a metaphorical kick in the teeth, so she nodded, gave a wan smile and stepped onto the floor with him, hoping that he may have seen sense. She was wrong.

"What the fuck do you think you're playing at," he hissed as they joined the dancers. She looked into his hate-filled angry eyes and immediately tried to pull away from him, but he gripped her tightly and pulled her close to him.

"Don't you know he's only taking a hand outta' ye. He wants into your knickers just to spite me, if he hasn't already got there."

She struggled to get away, but he gripped her more tightly, her discomfort unnoticed in the throng of dancers, and he apparently smiling as he whispered his vitriol into her ear. Her fears magnified. He was wildly jealous or quite mad. She glanced around looking frantically for Dan but he wasn't to be seen. She kicked Owen hard on the shin and he stepped back with a muttered curse, looked murderously at her and walked off to the back of the hall while she stumbled, heart racing, over to Paddy's bar table.

He stared at her. "You look a bit off, are you ok?"

"Yes...no...I'm not Paddy. Owen..."

"Making a nuisance of himself again I suppose. Here, knock this back," he handed her a glass of brandy, which she drank quickly, causing her to gasp and choke as the fiery liquid hit the back of her throat.

The dance ended and Dan escorted Grace to her seat and looking around he spotted Siobhan at the bar and made his way over to her. He was smiling until he got close and saw her face, straining to hold back tears. He knew immediately the cause of the tension, looked hard at her and said "Owen?" She nodded.

He took her hands and spoke with the look of a man who had done enough pussyfooting,

"I'm going to sort that bastard out once and for all."

Paddy put his hand on Dan's shoulder. "That wouldn't be wise Dan, and anyway he's away. I saw him leave a couple of minutes ago."

"Well, he gone and spoiled a great night, for us anyway. The bastard's mad Paddy, and that makes him dangerous."

"Ah, he's not a bad lad at heart. Just a bit tunnel-visioned when it comes to his wants and needs. He pays no notice to people's feelings."

"Paddy, he needs psychiatric help. There's a mental hospital in Letterkenny I believe. Any chance of getting him to go for treatment?"

"Aw jasus, that would be a hard one to organize. How would you persuade him that he needs help? Sure, a madman doesn't know he's mad. You would need four or five strong men to hold him down and tie him up and take him by boat and car to Letterkenny. Can't see that happenin'."

"It's a tough one alright Paddy. Pour me a brandy if you would. Siobhan?"

She shook her head "One was enough thanks. Can we go soon? I'm not sure I can keep a happy face on for the rest of the night."

"Yeah, we'll go, and I'm gonna have a serious talk with Mr. Owen Gallagher tomorrow."

The next dance struck up, Dan finished his drink and he and Siobhan made their way smiling and nodding out to the porch. They donned their wet-weather gear and pushed the door open against the wind and stepped out into the dark night, the continuing gale, the wind whipping their coats around their legs, the rain stinging their faces. The street was deserted as they fought their way arm in arm towards Siobhan and Grace's house on the far edge of the town.

They didn't notice that they were being followed.

CHAPTER TWELVE

CONFRONTATION

Over a steaming mug of tea and a piece of fruit cake, Siobhan told Dan about her encounter with Owen, but not in his crude language. Dan sat leaning forward, his left elbow on the edge of the sofa, fingers to his forehead, looking into the dying embers of the turf fire, sipping his tea. Neither spoke as they listened to the wind whistling around the gutters and downpipes, making the discordant sounds of the woodwind section tuning up before a concert. The rain battered the windows in intermittent squalls.

"I think I know what happened to Richard, Siobhan. I think we've all known it all the time but were afraid to voice it. Since you told me about Owen, and from the first time I met him I could see we were dealing with an irrational dangerous man. Now what? I don't know. It could have been his jealousy of Richard and his fear of losing you that, oh darling I'm sorry,"

Siobhan gave a little wail and sobbed, “That’s my biggest fear. That I was to blame for Richard’s disappearance, maybe even his death.”

Dan drew her to him and wrapped his arms around her, his head against hers. “How can it be your fault my love. If Richard is safe somewhere and left the island in a hurry, maybe because of Owen, that would be the best outcome. We still don’t know if the two men who came to visit him had anything to do with his disappearance, although from what you said about them and the fact that they seemed to be known here and liked, kinda rules them out, in the meantime that is. If Owen killed Richard, how can you be to blame?”

“Because if I hadn’t been friendly with Richard and made Owen jealous...”

“So, you plan to go around for the rest of your life afraid to smile at a man in case Owen attacks him?”

She smiled wanly. “I had had enough of Owen and I was going to leave the island earlier than planned and head home, but I knew in my heart that he would follow me. I would need to go somewhere, probably abroad, to escape him. And then you arrived and something made me want to stay here a little longer.”

He turned his head and looked into her eyes, “I’m glad you stayed.”

“But I was afraid for you, as you may have gathered. And my fears are coming true. You’re the object of his hate now, and once again it’s all my fault,” she sobbed, “I don’t want anything to happen to you Dan, oh God I’m afraid,” she gripped his hands fiercely.

“I’ll be careful, don’t worry.” He looked at his watch. “Crikey, it’s three o’clock. I hate leaving you, but it’s time to get to bed.”

“You could stay here, on the sofa if you wished. It’s an awful night.” She raised her face to his and looked into his eyes, her expression giving the lie to her suggestion that he sleep on the sofa.

"A very tempting offer Miss Gray. But Grace will be home shortly I expect, and your reputation would be destroyed if it was known that I stayed here. Also, if I was missing from my bed in Keenan's people might think that another visitor had gone missing and spark a search, and I don't want to do that to them."

"Of course, you're right Dan. Bugger off then," she laughed and slapped him on the shoulder

"And don't expect to get that offer again!"

Dan stuck his arm in the air and waggled it. "Oh, please teacher, please teacher, Siobhan Gray said a bad word and she's being rude as well," he laughed and jumped to his feet and put on his damp coat. "Now, when I go, don't open the door to anyone. Grace has her own key?"

"Of course."

"Good. Then I'm off, but before I go," he leaned in and kissed her, quietly and gently at first, but she responded passionately and hugged him fiercely. He eventually pulled back from her.

"Any more of that and you're in trouble young lady," he smiled, his heart thumping.

"That sort of trouble might be welcome, if I found the right man," she smiled, "please take care. Here, take this wee torch to light your way."

"G'night sweet lady. See you tomorrow," he closed the door behind him and walked into the whistling wind and blustery rain and headed back to the village, smiling to himself at the wonder of his feelings for Siobhan, and better, having them reciprocated.

It seemed that the celebrations were continuing in the hall as the street ahead was still deserted. After about a hundred yards from Siobhan's he reached the first building at the edge of the village which was an old deserted roofless house. Suddenly a figure loomed out of the darkness startling him and blocking his way. He instinctively jumped back and shone the weak light at the drenched crouching figure in front of him.

"Owen!"

"Yes, it's me, who the fuck did you expect?" he yelled into the wind. "I've been here for a fucking hour while you were in that bitch's house. Did you have a good ride then? I warned you. I warned her. Why won't she do what she's told. None of yiz will listen. Ye have destroyed my life."

His voice got louder as his rant continued. "There's only one way to deal with you, you bastards who come here and screw our women, and you wouldn't be the first to try to take her from me."

Dan spoke, his voice shaking, "You mean Richard Hilliard?"

"That's just the fucker I mean, he tried it too, but I sorted him. Now it's your turn, bastard."

A raging Dan lunged forward towards Owen who stepped to the side and swung his hand which was clutching a small rock, and caught Dan on the side of the head stunning him. He fell to the muddy roadway. As if in a dream he saw a blurred Owen standing over him with a large rock in his two hands about to smash his skull when a loud bang momentarily drowned out the noise of the storm and Owen fell on top of him, the rock he was holding glancing off Dan's head. Dan passed out.

As consciousness slowly returned, he heard voices and twisted his head about.

"It's OK Dan, it's over."

He heard Siobhan's voice. He looked up to see her with a

bloodied handkerchief dabbing at his bleeding head which was resting on her lap. It was still raining and he felt the weight of coats covering him.

"Where's Owen?" he gasped, trying to rise to his feet, but she stopped him and whispered in his ear. "Owen has been shot Dan, he's dead."

Owen dead? How? That loud bang. Who? My coat will be destroyed in this mud. His thoughts were fragmented and he was trying to make sense of the scene around him and the blurry images that crossed his vision. He became aware of other people and just a few feet away from him, a weeping Madge was sitting by the body of her son with Fr. Tom whispering the Last Rites into his ear. The rain stopped and the wind lessened. He saw people he didn't know and some he recognised. Peter was there carrying a lantern, and Paddy, and Sean Mary, John Keenan and several other islanders. Dan struggled to rise. He was still in a state of unreality and shock. Silently Siobhan and Paddy helped him to his feet. It still seemed like a bad dream. Grace arrived on the scene and she and Siobhan put each of his arms around their shoulders and headed slowly back towards their house. Dan stopped after a minute and turned to look at the scene of the confrontation.

The sad cortege of islanders was heading back to the village with four of the men carrying Owen, his weeping mother walking beside her son holding his hand, Fr. Tom on the other side, and Peter walking in front and holding the lantern high to show the way. A faint light appeared on the horizon as the two little groups made their way homeward.

CHAPTER THIRTEEN

BACK TO AUSTRALIA

Two weeks later Paddy and Bella were preparing to open the pub, when the door opened and Fr. Tom and Sean Mary Doohan came in. Paddy smiled at the two men.

"Ah good morning gentlemen. We are honoured, Bella, to have Church and State visiting our humble establishment. Is it too early to offer you a drink?"

"It's a bit early Paddy, but I'm sure Sean Mary wouldn't say no to a cup of tea, and neither would I. Is the kettle boiling Bella?"

"No problem Father. Milk and sugar for both?"

"Milk and one sugar for me please."

"Just milk for me," said Sean Mary.

It was a nice morning, but cool, and the fire had just been lit. Paddy never liked the look of a dead fireplace, and unless it was very warm outside, the pub fire was always burning cheerfully.

"C'mon over to the fire gentlemen. She should be giving out some heat shortly."

The three men sat on the cushioned seats and stretched their legs out in front of them. It was obvious to Paddy that they were here to see Dan off on his return to Australia, but that they needed to speak to him before he left, and that it was going to be difficult. Paddy opened up the conversation.

"Well, that was quite a bit of Garda activity here over the last two weeks, and I never saw so many newspaper and radio reporters in me life, they were trippin' over one another. They didn't do me business any harm, but I'm glad to see the back of them. I hear the guards turned over every rock on the island looking for the murder weapon. They certainly quizzed me and everybody else on the island, and almost all our visitors who were here for the election. Did they find out anythin' I wonder?"

Fr. Tom looked sideways at him. "C'mon now Paddy. Did you expect them to?"

"Well... not really Father."

Bella arrived with two mugs of tea and a plate of biscuits on a small tray. "Here we are. Tea for two. Did you want a cup Daddy?"

"Ah sure I might as well, thanks."

She went back into the kitchen.

"Well, Sean, you had an eventful start to your reign!"

"I surely did Paddy, and I could have done without it. I hope to God it never happens again. Two killings inside a few weeks, imagine."

Fr. Tom looked sad. "It might have been three Sean. I wonder if people will shun Inishard now, will people be put off coming here? What sort of people will they think we are anyway?"

Paddy snorted. "If I know people, they'll flock here to stare at us and wonder. When this story dies down, we'll need to watch, as some reporter will come sneaking in and want the 'inside' story for a good bundle of money. We must remember that. Not that anyone who knows anything is stupid enough to do that, but be must always be aware that it could be tried."

Bella arrived back. "Here y'are Dad. I suppose ye are here to see Dan off Father."

"We are indeed Bella. Mr. Livings... I mean Mr. Hilliard, as you know, is off this morning, back to Australia. It's an awful thing that happened to his brother, and nearly happened to himself. His family has little reason to think kindly on Inishard. Poor Owen. There was no hope for Owen."

Bella sat down and there was a silence as they thought about Owen. Then she piped up, "Ah, it's not all bad. I think that Dan has got something good from his visit here. I'm talking about Siobhan, as if you didn't know. He was interested in me at the start you know, but I'm far too young for him."

Paddy and Sean rolled their eyes and Fr. Tom smiled, "Of course you are Bella."

The door latch clacked open and in walked Siobhan and Dan carrying his suitcase. They all got to their feet and went forward to welcome the newcomers with handshakes and nervous bonhomie.

Paddy made his usual friendly offer. "Would ye like a drink, or will ye settle for tea like the rest of us, tea Godsavus!"

Dan, who still had some stitches on his temple courtesy of Grace's medical kit thanked Paddy very much and indicated that tea would be good. Bella disappeared into the kitchen.

Fr. Tom ushered them over to the fire and opened the conversation rather nervously. "So, you're off today, Dan. Well, eh, we're sorry to see you go, and, eh, it was a terrible thing that happened, and eh, we hope you'll come back, and eh, oh for heaven's sakes, for a man who's never lost for a word, I'm bletherin' like an idiot. There are things I must say to you. Sean, Paddy, would you mind leaving me for a few minutes with Dan. Tell Bella to hold the tea."

"Of course, Father," they rose and went into the bar kitchen.

"Siobhan, would you stay please, I think you should hear what I have to say to Dan." He cleared his throat and began slowly. "Under normal circumstances the King would deal with the day-to-day matters of the island, but this is not a day-to-day matter, and so he has asked me to speak to you on his behalf." He paused, gathering his thoughts and continued, as Dan and Siobhan sat quietly, expectantly. "A terrible thing happened here recently, of which you and we are all painfully aware. Richard disappeared. He came to Inishard as a perfectly innocent visitor, and he was murdered. The islanders felt that they knew what happened him, but they had no proof. You see Dan, they have their own code of justice, their own beliefs, their own way of dealing with things. Twentieth century law has made few inroads here, yet. I do my best to persuade them to hand over certain matters to the Gardaí, but they haven't much faith in the forces of law and order when they see what passes as justice meted out in mainland courts. And there are times, God forgive me, when I think they may be right. Anyway, what I'm trying to say is, in their minds justice has been done in this case. They hope you think so too," he stared hopefully into Dan's eyes.

Dan nodded. "I do Fr. Tom," he smiled and stretched his hand out to the priest who took it warmly and gratefully, relaxing at Dan's reply. He shuddered to think of the consequences of any other response.

"At first Father, I wondered if the two men who came

from the mainland to speak to Richard had anything to do with his disappearance. Do you know who they were?"

"I do of course. They're from the IRA, Peadar O'Donnell and Liam Brady. They usually like to have a chat with strangers to suss out whether or not they might be British spies. You see, there are people who still object to the presence of the British in Ireland and who'll never rest till Ireland is free, but that's another long story we haven't time to get into. It wouldn't have taken them long to work out that Richard was no spy."

"Another question, if I may. Who saved my life? Who shot Owen?"

There was a troubled silence as the priest formulated his reply. "We all did Dan, all of us. We're all responsible. Naturally they didn't tell me about their thoughts or plans, as I would have done my best as a priest to stop them. They saw what had happened, they saw what might happen and they were prepared to take steps to prevent that. By my silence I am just as guilty as everyone else, as I knew in my heart what the solution might be, and I did nothing." He dropped his head.

Siobhan reached out and took the priest's hands in hers. "You're being too hard on yourself Father Tom. You're being wise after the event. Just know that the people love you, but there was nothing you could do to stop island justice. If Owen could have been stopped any other way, that's what would have happened, but he was about to kill Dan, so..."

Fr. Tom raised Siobhan's hands to his lips and smiled at her. "Isn't it strange though, that Richard's disappearance might never have been proved Dan, if it wasn't for your coming here and becoming another man standing in the way of Owen's plans."

Siobhan took Dan's hand in hers. Dan had one more question, "What does Madge think of this form of justice?"

"Ah, sure what can she think, the creatur. She has lost a husband and now a son God help her. A problem son, but the fruit of her womb. He has caused her a lot of pain and heartbreak."

As if on cue, the door opened again and Madge and Peter stepped slowly into the pub and hearing the door opening, the others came from the kitchen. Fr. Tom, Dan and Siobhan stood up and they all stared at her, but her eyes were only on Dan's face. Then as she spoke, she burst into tears.

"Mr Hilliard, oh Mr. Hilliard. I'm very, very sorry for all this. Can you ever forgive us?"

Dan walked over to her and put his arms around her and held her tightly then looked deeply into her eyes. "It's alright Madge. It's alright, everything's alright. I have nothing to forgive you for. We all have crosses to bear and we've both had our share of heartbreak. We mustn't let this thing destroy us. We should remember the good days and smile. We must get on with our lives, looking forward. Other people need us."

At his words, Madge sobbed and hugged Dan. The men were moved and coughed and blew their noses, as they struggled to keep the tears from their eyes as they watched and listened. Siobhan and Bella didn't even try to hold back their tears. Then Madge reached up and kissed Dan on the cheek. "Thank you, Mr. Hilliard, you don't know what your words mean to me."

"Madge, enough of this Mr. Hilliard. Dan please. Now say it."

She laughed through her tears, "Thank you - Dan."

"That's better. Now Peter, c'mere," a beaming Peter was grabbed and hugged. With a flourish Peter brought a paper bag from behind his back and diving his hand in, he produced his home-made aeroplane which Dan had admired.

"F-for you Dan," he said shyly.

Dan was really touched and thanked him very much. "It'll

take pride of place on my mantelpiece at home and remind me of my first friend here, Peter Gallagher, the man who introduced me to a certain school-teacher."

Peter wriggled with embarrassment and pleasure as everyone applauded him.

"I don't think it'll come as any surprise to you if I tell you that Siobhan and I will be married. I could see that on our first meeting she was smitten with me and shortly after she begged me to marry her. Now, I can't resist a woman's tears, so I said yes, and here we are."

Dan backed up and held Peter in front of him as a shield as Siobhan advanced glaring at him, and laughter filled the space of the earlier tension. The two were surrounded with smiling faces and congratulations as Grace walked in. "What's goin' on?"

Bella gave her the good news.

"Is that all? Sure, that was obvious from day one. I knew somethin' was goin' on when one day the door of the house opened and Siobhan floated in with a faraway look in her eyes."

Siobhan blushed.

Paddy jumped up on a chair. "This is great news altogether. Bella, get rid of the tea and produce the sparkling wine, we have no champagne. and early or not, we're going to drink to Dan and Siobhan's engagement. Peter, give her a hand."

Through the window they could see what looked like the whole population standing on the pier, very quiet and restrained as they waited to bid farewell to the man whose brother was murdered on their island. Sean Mary spoke up, "If you'll excuse me, I'll just go and have a word with them. They don't know how the land lies and it's not fair to keep them wonderin'."

"Do that Sean," said Fr. Tom. Bella and Peter handed out

the glasses of sparkling wine to everyone and they all toasted Dan and Siobhan.

"On behalf of my fiancée and myself, thank you all very much for your good wishes. Now, I have to go back to Australia and talk to my parents and to see to some business affairs. But I'll be back in about a month and I hope to persuade my folks to come with me to meet you all. Father, we want you to marry us then. Paddy, will you be our best man?"

"I'd be honoured Dan."

Siobhan broke in, "I already have one bridesmaid," she smiled at Grace, "and I was wondering Bella if you would do us the honour of being a bridesmaid as well?"

"Me? Jeepers. I'd love it, thanks a million." She wondered if she could invite Albert.

Dan continued, "And Peter, we'd like you, along with the King, to be our guests of honour. Ah don't be so worried looking, you won't have anything to do. And now, my vessel awaits and I must away."

They all trooped out through the door and down through the smiling applauding crowd on the pier to where the half-decker sat ticking over, awaiting its passenger.

EPILOGUE

There y'are now. A story of love, of hate, of death, of forgiveness, all on my own little island of Inishard. The recent events will never be forgotten of course, but things have returned to a semblance of normality, thank God. Dan is expected back shortly and his parents are coming too. As you can imagine the girls, Siobhan, Grace and Bella are up to high doh organising their dresses and hairdos and all that stuff and the people are planning a great welcome for the Hilliard family to try to make up for...well, you know!

My name is Liam McClafferty. I used to be the King here, and I like to keep a distant eye on things, you know how it is.

DID YOU ENJOY THIS STORY?

If you enjoyed Troubled Island, please let W.M. know by leaving him a review. Thank you.

ABOUT THE AUTHOR

W.M. (Billy) Patterson lives in Donegal. He is best known as a member of the internationally acclaimed family Folk group The Pattersons in the 1960's and '70's. Latterly he was a founder member of and a broadcaster with Highland Radio in Letterkenny. He directed and performed many roles in musicals from Gilbert & Sullivan to Jesus Christ Superstar with Letterkenny Musical Society, as well as directing a professional version of Hansel and Gretel.

This is his second story after 'Robert's War', which follows the adventures of a member of the SOE in WW2.

Manufactured by Amazon.ca
Acheson, AB

34960129R00063